Tales of the Natural and the Supernatural

Bibhutibhushan Bandyopadhyay (1894–1950), the author of eighteen novels and nearly two hundred and fifty stories, is indisputably one of Bengal's greatest and most loved writers, and a principal architect of modern Bangla fiction and realism. A master wordsmith, with an equal gift for both the novel and the short story, his works have been widely translated and adapted for the small and big screen, most famously, his first novel *Pather Panchali* and its sequel *Aparajito*, by Satyajit Ray. Deeply lyrical, with a profound empathy for all facets of life and the living, and a sharp eye for the extraordinary in the guise of the ordinary, his other well-known works include *Aranyak*, *Adarsha Hindu Hotel*, *Debjan*, *Ashani Sanket*, and *Chander Pahar*.

Debashish Sen is a writer, translator, and a literary scholar specialising in nineteenth-century English literature, with an interest in the psychoanalytic study of novels and fictional characters. He is the author of *Psychological Realism in 19th Century Fiction: Studies in Turgenev, Tolstoy, Eliot and Brontë*.

Tathagata Banerjee is Associate Professor of English Literature at Bangabasi College, under the University of Calcutta, and a literary critic, writer and translator of Bangla fiction. He is the grandson of Bibhutibhushan Bandyopadhyay.

Tales of the Natural and the Supernatural

Bibhutibhushan Bandyopadhyay

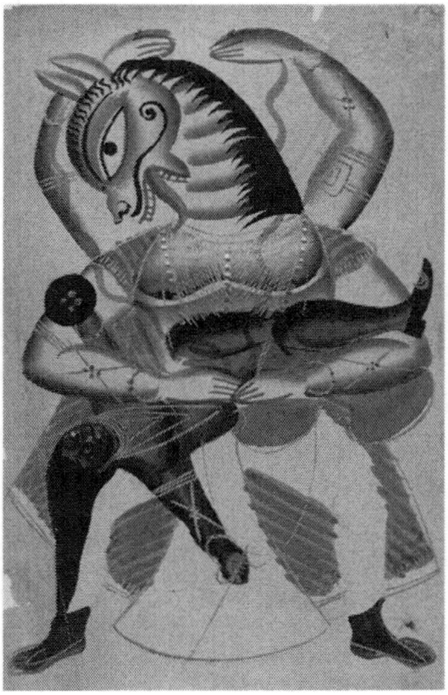

Translated from the original Bengali by

Debashish Sen

With a Foreword by

Tathagata Banerjee

Orient BlackSwan

TALES OF THE NATURAL AND THE SUPERNATURAL

ORIENT BLACKSWAN PRIVATE LIMITED

Registered Office
3-6-752 Himayatnagar, Hyderabad 500 029, Telangana, India
e-mail: centraloffice@orientblackswan.com

Other Offices
Bengaluru, Chennai, Guwahati, Hyderabad, Kolkata,
Mumbai, New Delhi, Noida, Patna

First published by Orient Blackswan Private Limited 2021

The images used herein are anonymous artworks from the nineteenth-century Kalighat school of painting in West Bengal, as available in the public domain.

ISBN 978-93-5442-094-8

041726

Typeset in
Dante MT Std 11/13.5 *by*
Le Studio Graphique, Gurgaon 122 007

Printed in India at
Replika Press Pvt. Ltd., Kundli Sonepat 131 028, Haryana.

Published by
Orient Blackswan Private Limited
3-6-752 Himayatnagar, Hyderabad 500 029, Telangana, India
e-mail: info@orientblackswan.com

Contents

Foreword — *vii*
Tathagata Banerjee
Translator's Note — *xi*
Note on Pronunciation — *xv*

A Strange Malady — 1
Kashinath's Tale — 8
A Day — 17
The Tiger Mantra — 22
Master Vidhu — 32
The Medal — 39
The Mountains of Kushal — 53
The Bodiless — 62
Grandma — 72
A Mystery — 83
The Hunter — 90
Illusion — 99
Ghost — 112
In the Jungle of Bomaiburu — 118
Doctor Moni — 127
The Intoxicant — 143

Glossary — 151

Foreword

Bibhutibhushan Bandyopadhyay made his name as a novelist when, in 1929, the publication of his debut novel *Pather Panchali* shot him to fame almost overnight. Today, it is mainly on the strength of his eighteen novels that he is considered one of the principal architects of modern Bangla fiction. Several highly acclaimed movies and TV series, including four major films by Satyajit Ray, were created from some of these works. Unfortunately, all this has somewhat eclipsed Bibhutibhushan's excellence as a writer of short stories, especially among those who do not read Bangla natively.

Bibhutibhushan wrote nearly two hundred and fifty stories, which include the very first and the last of his published works. Over the span of his career, which lasted about twenty-eight years, he explored a great variety of themes and styles. The sixteen narratives in the present collection can be said to belong to two or three loose thematic groups, which I will try to describe. I say 'loose' because many of these stories defy neat assignment to any one group.

Clearly, the translator is fond of ghost stories, because his selection of sixteen contains nine tales of the supernatural. Bibhutibhushan is among the prominent writers of the modern Bangla ghost story, a genre that has flourished since the late nineteenth century. The events of his life seem to suggest that he became attracted to spiritualism and theosophy after the untimely passing of his first wife in his youth, about a year after their marriage. He was a deeply religious man, though not in any conventional sense. Although religiosity does not necessarily imply belief in life after death, Bibhutibhushan seems to have believed in it, if we accept his unusual novel *Debjaan* as an expression of his faith. There, the protagonist dies within the first few pages, and the rest of the book shows his afterlife and interactions with the world of the living.

Of the nine stories, 'Maya' (translated as 'Illusion') is certainly the most remarkable, and perhaps one of the most striking supernatural tales in any language. It is the story of a man who gradually falls under the spell of a haunted house with a difference. The author's mastery is revealed in how he uses the first-person point of view to convey the narrator's descent into captivity, and maybe also insanity. Here Bibhutibhushan draws upon the venerable tradition of haunted house stories, but many readers have felt that he improves upon his predecessors, including Rabindranath Tagore, whose 'Kshudhita Pashan' ('The Hungry Stones') inaugurated the form in Bangla in 1895. 'Maya' proposes that the phenomena we often interpret as supernatural could have their origin in other dimensions inhabited by creatures normally invisible to us (and we to them). This is an uncommon idea for the second quarter of the twentieth century, showing Bibhutibhushan's acquaintance with science fiction and perhaps the writings of H. P. Lovecraft.

'The Medal' belongs with a number of stories (of which this is the only representative in this collection) that Bibhutibhushan wrote about haunted or accursed objects. 'The Bodiless' is about a guardian spirit. Our family tradition has it that it is based on an actual experience of Bibhutibhushan's father-in-law (my grandmother's father), who had a transferable job in the government's excise department. 'In the Jungle of Bomaiburu' is a tale of lycanthropy, a rare instance in Bangla literary fiction. It is not a stand-alone story, but an episode excerpted from the celebrated novel *Aranyak*, which was based on Bibhutibhushan's sojourn as an absentee landlord's revenue officer in a remote area in Bihar. He probably wrote it down as he heard it from one of the forest dwellers who became his friends.

Three stories involve hunting, and two of them, 'The Tiger Mantra' and 'The Intoxicant', contain supernatural elements. The first is a children's perennial favourite, although not specifically written for them. Bibhutibhushan was interested in the Sundarbans, and especially the ruined and overgrown fortifications that lie hidden there, relics of the Barabhuiyans from the sixteenth and seventeenth centuries. 'The Tiger Mantra' lightly touches upon this theme. There is another story in a similar setting called 'Abhishapta' ('The Accursed'), which in my opinion is superior to this one in its atmosphere and historical depth, but it is not included here. 'The Intoxicant' is set in Rajasthan, and the characters, too, are natives of that state. There is no evidence that Bibhutibhushan ever set foot there, so it may be assumed that it was adapted entirely from an oral source.

Disempowered characters are a staple of Bibhutibhushan's fiction, and their frequent occurrence often coincides with instances of desolation, desertion, dereliction and abandonment. A number of stories here illustrate this point, but none so powerfully as 'Doctor Moni', which is about a rural quack who fails at everything he does, yet keeps trying in the hope of a better tomorrow. This and 'Grandma' take us back to an age when the rural population of Bengal was getting depleted as many people gave up agriculture and related livelihoods and moved to urban centres. 'Ghost' shows us from a child's point of view the solitary end that inevitably awaits the utterly disenfranchised and truly forsaken.

Debashish Sen has done an admirable job of translating the flavour and pitch of Bibhutibhushan's short fiction. I heartily recommend this volume to all who are unable to read the originals. Much of this phenomenal author's work remains untranslated; perhaps the present effort will encourage others to fill the gap.

Tathagata Banerjee

Translator's Note

Bibhutibhushan Bandyopadhyay, perhaps more than any other writer in Bengali literature, succeeded in transmitting his worldview and the beauty of his thoughts to his readers. For someone who had never really set out to be a writer, the range of his creative achievements is indeed remarkable. One only needs to read his short stories and novels to realise that he excelled at both—a rare quality amongst writers. Many who have understood and loved his works recognise that he was one writer who should have won the Nobel Prize but never did.

Bibhutibhushan had two passions in life—the human being and nature—and he wrote with great intensity about both. He believed that there should never be a disconnect between the two. As many of his works amply indicate, Bibhutibhushan was a lover of the natural world. 'I am most happy,' he wrote to a friend, 'when I am in a lonely primeval forest.'

As the name of this bouquet of stories indicates, they deal with the natural and the supernatural. Bibhutibhushan believed that life's true essence lay in appreciating and honouring nature and its abundant riches. 'The significance of life lies,' he wrote, 'not in earning money and name and fame, not in gaining praise and the gratification of desires, but in realising the depths of life, in the joy of attempting to understand the mystery of the universe.' Bibhutibhushan explored as much of the world as he could, spending years in the midst of nature. He realised that the sounds of the forest did more good to the soul of a person than the noise of the city. 'The forest reveals the real India,' he wrote, 'for our civilisation grew in the peace of the forest, as did the *Veda*s and the *Aranyak Upanishads*. It all happened in the depth of the forest silence, and not in the crowded cities.' His travels in the countryside and the experiences they brought found their way into his writing. If it be said that a writer writes from experience and imagination then it is evident that Bibhutibhushan made ample use of both. His works leave the reader with the message that 'if you immerse yourself deeply in nature, she will shower on you joy, happiness, beauty and peace.'

But human beings are an inherent part of nature and Bibhutibhushan excelled also in the depiction of their everyday struggles, their innermost thoughts and desires, subtle shades of feeling, and those rare yet perfectly natural sensations. His works salute the spirit of common people, describing their daily toil, their simple joys and their experience of life and all that it brings—loneliness, loss, pain, unfulfilled needs and desires, and the inevitable tragedies. The reader will find stories in this collection that are based in urban areas and will be able to appreciate the nuances in the author's depiction of the city and urban life.

Then there are the supernatural stories. It will interest the reader to know that ghosts have been an important part of the folklore and socio-cultural fabric of Bengal. Supernatural entities have formed the plots for many well-loved short stories and novels in Bengali literature. It should then not be surprising that this was one of Bibhutibhushan's favourite themes. Bibhutibhushan's supernatural fiction may sometimes have subtle elements of the paranormal, and the buildup tends to keep the reader engrossed. Another quality in his writings is that his narrative style can sometimes seem more spoken than written, and this inevitably draws the reader into the story almost conversationally. Conventionally realistic aspects of life are almost always woven into the story in such a manner that even after the tale has been told it leaves the reader ample food for thought and contemplation. Of course, the feeling of suspense and trepidation remain thick in the air.

In some places words from the source language have been preserved in this translation. This has been done primarily for two reasons. Firstly, it is not always feasible to translate every word into another language, especially where it will end up distorting the original meaning of the text or conveying only half of it. To faithfully convey the writer's message to the reader, and to aid the integrity of the reading experience, I felt it was better to include the original term with an explanation of it in English. Secondly, I must confess that there were terms that could have been translated into English, but I chose not to do so. This has been inspired by a desire to preserve the socio-cultural and ethno-linguistic background of the stories, which I hope will ultimately lead to a better reading experience and understanding of this work. The reader will also notice that the glossary is fairly detailed. To anyone familiar with Bibhutibhushan's writings it is evident that he had a wide range of interests and possessed a deep love of knowledge and a curious bent of mind. I believe he would have wanted his readers to take away more from the stories than just the 'stories' themselves.

My thanks go to the author the beauty of whose writing made me want to translate his stories into English. I would like to express my gratitude to my parents—my father, Late Churamoni Sen and my mother, Krishna Sen—who kept Bengal alive within me even though I grew up away from it. Thanks to my sister Joyshri who first inspired in me the habit of reading literature and with whom I spent countless evenings listening to our father as he read out fascinating stories in the Bengali language. Heartfelt thanks to Tathagata Banerjee, Bibhutibhushan Bandyopadhyay's grandson, for giving his valuable suggestions, and for kindly contributing the Foreword to this collection. Many thanks to Vidya Rao of Orient BlackSwan, for taking interest in this project, guiding me through the publication process, and helping this book see the light of day. I would like to thank Amitabha Gupta and my wife, Sonal for encouraging my studies in the Bengali language. Thanks to my little son, Mrigankashekhar for allowing me to pursue my academic interests in spite of the time it takes me away from him.

Note on Pronunciation

There are several words in the book that have been spelt with a single ***a*** which in actual speech are pronounced with a long ***aa*** sound as in *bath*, *father*, etc. The spelling has been simplified within the text to ensure ease of reading. Thus, Goyalb*a*gi should be pronounced Goyalb*aa*gi. The words are mainly names of places and people, words for flora and fauna, official designations and items of food and daily use. The words are listed below on the left, with their pronunciations on the right.

aloo bhat	aloo bhaat
ameen	aameen
amrra	aamrraa
Anadi Mama	Anaadi Mama
Bagh-Anchra	Baagh-Aanchraa
Bauri Bagan	Bauri Bagaan
Bejerdanga	Bejerdaangaa
Bomaiburu	Bomaaiburu
Bonkati	Bonkaati
Borjor Nala	Borjor Naalaa
dafadar	dafadaar
golpata	golpaataa
goran	goraan
Goyalbagi	Goyalbaagi
Hatol Badiyar	Haatol Baadiyaar
hetal	hetaal

Jhanpri-shol	Jhaanpri-shol
Kakdangar	Kaakdaangaar
kalmegh	kaalmegh
KalRanghat	KaalRanghaat
Kanai	Kaanaai
Katchuri	Kaatchuri
Kobiraj	Kobiraaj
madar	maadaar
Magniram	Maagniraam
Mahadal	Mahadaal
Manganbera	Maanganberaa
Marang-Bonga	Maarang-Bongaa
nagra	naagraa
Nahara Nipat	Nahaaraa Nipat
Nankansbahal	Naankaansbahaal
oler danta	oler daantaa
Panikar	Paanikar
Pankhola	Paankholaa
Rakhal Master	Raakhaal Master
shankha	shaankhaa
tandav	taandav

A Strange Malady

I'd taken the train that goes from Goyari towards Krishnanagar to reach a relative's house. Once you get down at Bagula station, there is a straight concrete path that leads to Krishnanagar. Post-noon found me walking alone on this path towards my destination; there was hardly anyone to be seen on the way. It was the monsoon season, and dark clouds hovered over the skyline. The air was heavy with moisture-laden winds blowing over the land. Droplets of water fell incessantly from the huge, dense trees lining both sides of the road. The day was cold, albeit suitable for covering distances on foot.

I'd left behind Domchiti and Goyalbagi; both sides of the road lined with dense, wild trees; another eight–ten miles to go before I reached my destination. Looking for some rest, I'd just seated myself on a paved footbridge, when another traveller of the road appeared and seated himself on the opposite side. After some time, he glanced in my direction and subsequently addressing me in a hesitant manner, said: 'Sir, would you happen to have a match?' After helping himself to a matchstick he said, 'Would you like a bit of tobacco? I have some in my pouch, and I can prepare it for you.'

I replied, 'No, thanks. I don't need...'

The refusal seemed to sadden my fellow-traveller.

'Why not, dear sir? Do have some. I'll prepare it for you.' The manner in which he said this seemed as though there could be no happiness for him if I disallowed him from preparing tobacco for me. Taken aback, I glanced at him—a man unknown to me, a complete stranger—and wondered how on earth it could possibly make a difference to him whether or not I shared his tobacco?

I assented.

I was able to observe him well now. He was below thirty, with a youthful face and long hair, and he wore a khaki shirt. But it was the eyes that drew one's attention—so peaceful and so innocent were they, that looking at them one could not possibly suspect or mistrust him. A broken umbrella and a small bundle were his accoutrements; in clothes and manner he came across as an inveterate wanderer. From there on, the two of us began traversing the path together. Dusk was falling by the time we reached the bazaar of Mamudpur. We took shelter at a grocer's shop for the night, the reason being that everyone we encountered warned us that it was not a good time to travel. Once dusk had fallen, walking on that path wasn't without risk. Many a time, people were murdered on the way even for small amounts of money.

By this time, I'd had the chance to get to know my fellow-traveller better and we were on quite amicable terms. He was a Brahmin's son and belonged to some village in the district of Nadiya. He had no one left in his family and used to wander from one place to another. After spending a year wandering through good places and bad, he was now returning to his village.

There was one trait in particular that I observed in him, which was both strange and quite unique, a characteristic removed from what generally dwells in the common populace. He seemed to be forever seeking and striving for an opportunity to bestow a favour on his fellow beings. How he could make the person next to him happy was a fervent and ever-present desire, and the quest to fulfil this desire seemed to be almost an obsession with him!

He took upon himself the responsibility of preparing the evening's meal for the two of us; in no way would he condescend to let me help him even a little bit.

I began to eat, and it didn't take me long to realise that the man was an expert cook. In fact, saying that he was an expert cook wouldn't do him full justice. It would be more appropriate to say that as far as culinary art was concerned, he was an artist, and of the highest order, brimming with talent!

I was left feeling awestruck. 'Where on earth did you learn such magical cooking skills?' I asked him.

'No one taught me,' he replied. 'It simply grew on its own.'

'Given your culinary abilities, you could easily get a well-paying job in Calcutta or elsewhere, any day. Get hold of a rich, well-to-do household instead of wandering around in an unsettled manner.'

He laughed and replied, 'I've tried that. But there is a trait in me which makes me reluctant to accept any kind of employment anymore. You could even say it is a kind of a malady...a strange malady. Let me explain.

'After passing my matriculation exams I'd thought I would study further, but since my financial condition wasn't good enough to bear the cost of any further education, I had to give it a miss.

'So, I left home to look for a suitable job. Passing through a forested and mountainous area in the district of Singbhum, I came to know that somewhere nearby they were carrying out explorations for minerals. Wandering from one place to another, I finally reached the spot. What I saw was a huge plain with lots of tents and many people. I found myself a cook's job there in an overseer's tent-house. My employer was a man over forty, who stayed there alone with a boy servant. Once he had taken me in employment, he relieved this other fellow of his duties.

'After working there for some time, I noticed that a peculiar affection had taken root in my heart for my master. All my thoughts seemed to be directed towards making him happy. My only aim was to cook well and satisfy his palate. This tendency gradually took hold of me and became a propensity. In that wild, forested land edible food was not easy to come by. I used to travel long distances to reach remote villages and collect whatever fish and vegetables I could lay my hands on to take back with me to the tent-house and cook. I never ventured to tell my master from where I sourced all the food that I cooked for him. Given the meagre resources, I always tried the best I could to prepare the tastiest possible dishes, so that my master could have a good meal.

'It cannot be said that my master was necessarily a good man. He started defaulting in paying me my wages, even suspecting me occasionally of pocketing the money that was given to me for purchases. I never allowed myself to take all this to heart. Four months passed by in this manner. During that time, I hardly allowed myself any other thoughts or distractions, my only aim being to give my master two good meals by whatever possible means. Let me give you a few examples.

'Once I heard that on a mountain river called Mungli, the *Santhals* had made a small dam and were fishing for large prawns. In those parts, fish and prawns were a rare delicacy—not something one could obtain easily through the power of money. To procure those prawns, I walked seven miles on hard, sunbaked rocky paths and on my return prepared a meal to feed my master. I didn't venture to mention to him where I'd got them from.

'Owing to my culinary skills and my devotion to my master, my name soon became well-known in those survey areas. One cannot find a good Bengali cook in those parts; consequently, others started feeling jealous of my master's good fortune. Gradually people secretly started coming to me to try and make me switch camps. They offered me better emoluments and more facilities. But I didn't consent to leave. Mr Kanungo, the head of the survey-camp, even offered to pay me twenty rupees, in place of the seven that I was earning in my master's service. But in my mind, the convenience of money was never a criterion. At no time did I tell my master about these goings-on.

'Around five–six months later, my master started behaving strangely. He began to constantly scold and abuse me. Not that he didn't find fault with me earlier, but there used to be a limit to his abuse. However, since I'd persisted in his service for so long, he may have thought that I'd no other place to go to. Consequently, whenever he could, with good reason or without, he started abusing me incessantly.

'One day my master called me and said, "Why didn't you take care to store the potatoes in some sand? All of them have sprouted and got spoiled."

'Dusk was about to fall. I had just returned with oil and masalas from a shop half a mile away. I replied, "I had indeed stored them in sand. However, in the rainy season how can one prevent potatoes from sprouting even though you use sand?"

'My master suddenly lost his cool and yelled, "You scoundrel, you have the audacity to argue with me?" And saying this, he gave me two hard slaps and walked out in fury.

'The bottle of oil I was carrying fell from my hands and broke into pieces. My ears turned red with the insult and pain of the assault. I sat down right there and stared into emptiness for a long time.

'But you will be surprised when I tell you (I too found it strange at the time) that instead of anger and outrage at this ill-treatment, I felt sympathy for my master. I thought to myself, "Alas! The man doesn't realise that he will lose my services because of what he has done. I only need to send a message to Head Kanungo's tent. It is well-known that Kanungo and my master don't get along particularly well." And addressing him silently, I said, "Tomorrow onwards, cook for yourself and burn your hands—you won't be able to find another Bengali cook in these parts!"

'The more I thought along these lines, the more I felt sympathy and pity for my master. It was an amazingly beautiful feeling. It felt as if God had entered my soul! How troubled the man would be were I to leave him, and he lost my services because of his stupid ways. Thoughts like these melted my heart, and I forgot about the insult to me altogether.

'At eight in the evening, I started preparations for the night meal. I'd already made up my mind that I wouldn't leave my master.

'The groom, however, had secretly observed the beating that I'd received at the hands of my master. He related the incident to everybody around. As a result, from the morning onwards, people from Head Kanungo's camp alone made five visits to try and get me to switch loyalties.

'For the next three or four days, they troubled me no end. As soon as my master left, they would come—Head Kanungo's people, as well as others. They would tempt me with various offers and tried to get me worked up against my master.

'Then one day on my way back to the camp, I ran into Head Kanungo. He was on his way to work astride his horse. Catching sight of me, he said, "Hey! Listen...did my men come to meet you?"

'"Yes sir," I replied.

'"Then why don't you agree to come and work for me? I heard that you were beaten the other day. Such a shame! How are you still managing to serve him? Come away to me right away! What do you say?"

'I found myself in deep trouble. This was no orderly or servant—Head Kanungo *Babu* was himself asking me. How do I say "No" to him? Then an idea suddenly occurred to me.

'I said, "Sir, I will indeed come to you today. See! How needlessly he beat me that day..."

'"What actually happened?" he asked.

'"Nothing much really. I found his set of gold waistcoat-buttons lying on the floor one day. I kept them in my box thinking I would give them to my master when he returned. But somehow, I forgot about it that evening. Next morning, having realised that he had lost the buttons, he searched frantically for them everywhere in the tent house. I was away at the shop. He happened to look in my box, and found them there. When I returned from the shop, he shouted, 'You rascal! You stole my gold buttons and hid them in your box!' And overcome with mad fury, he started raining blows on me. But sir, the fact is that I didn't keep the buttons with me with the intention of stealing them."

'Head Kanungo's expressions had gradually started to change. He was a smart fellow. He realised that I must have kept the set in my box with the intention of stealing it! Under the circumstances, who would give me a place under their roof? Muttering, "Oh well, that's all right," he left the place and went his way.

'Within a day or two, the news that I'd hidden my master's gold buttons and had received a beating on being caught spread like wildfire. Thereafter, people stopped coming to lure me with offers of employment. Who would knowingly keep a thief under their roof?

'One day my master said to me, "What is this that I'm hearing? Did you tell Head Kanungo that you'd hidden my gold buttons and as a consequence of that, I beat you that day? Why did you say such a thing?"

'I told my master everything—that people would come to entice me with offers of employment that I never wanted. If I hadn't concocted the story, what else could I have said to Head Kanungo? If I hadn't said to him what I said, how could I have possibly extricated myself from that difficult situation?

'My master said, "You're a strange creature. I've never known anyone like you. Just so that you don't have to leave me, you brought your name to false slander? One's own brother or son wouldn't do such a thing. You are no ordinary person. Please don't work as a cook for me anymore. If I continue to make a cook out of you, it will be a crime on my part."

'I tried hard to make my master understand and see that I wasn't willing to leave him. But he begged me with folded hands and said, "Don't make me partake in this crime, please. You are not a person who should work as a cook. Whatever has happened cannot be undone...but I cannot knowingly let you work as my servant."

'I lost my job, and even though my master went around telling everybody that the story of my having stolen his buttons was false, nobody believed him. Instead, everyone thought that I'd lost my job because of that incident.

'When I took leave of my master, he gave me his watch-and-chain and fifty rupees. See—this is the same watch-and-chain that he gave me.

'But ever since then I've carried a pain in my heart. I wander from one place to another. I never took the job of a cook at anyone's house again. Neither will I do so in the future.'

Previously published in Bengali as '*Bayurog*' in *Bibhutibhushan Golpo Shomogro*.

Kashinath's Tale

I often see our village doctor Kashi, with a small bag in hand, passing by our house on his way to work. On asking him where he is off to, he might reply by saying, 'I'm going to check on a patient in Sanakpur, brother.'

One day he said, 'I'm going to see a patient in Naihati, and from there I will go on to Shyamnagar.'

'So you have a patient there as well?' I asked.

'Everywhere actually,' he replied. 'Twice a month I have to visit Calcutta.'

I felt like laughing. It has been a year since Kashi came over from East Bengal and settled here in the village. He lives in a single-roomed, tin-roofed house in the midst of a jungle—covered from view by the branches and leaves of mango trees. Sunlight can't enter the house during the day. I have seen his wife, with torn clothes on her person, sorting grains of rice. If indeed he is doing as well as he claims, how come his living conditions are so dismal?

One day towards the end of the summer season, dense clouds gathered in the sky and it looked like it would rain any moment. I saw Kashi, his bag in hand, swiftly making his way across the path in front of my house.

Calling out to him, I said, '*Kobiraj Moshai*, where are you off to? Looks like it's going to rain any minute now.'

Kashi came over to my verandah, took a seat and said, 'I was on my way to catch the train to Ranaghat, to visit a patient.'

'Who is the patient?'

'A *Madrasi* fellow. His leg has swollen up enormously; all the doctors have given up on him. He had it x-rayed three times. I told him I wouldn't need any x-rays. My hands themselves work like x-rays.'

I was amused. If he is really as talented as he claims to be, why has he made a tin-roofed house in the midst of the jungle his home? Will people start considering you a good village doctor just by listening to your tall tales!

'Do have some tea,' I said to him.

'Sure, brother. It is about to rain. I might as well wait here for some time.'

'So your practice has started doing really well now, hasn't it?' I commented.

'What growth will it see, brother? It is the same as it used to be. I treat through alternative means and Tantric practices. The ailments which none other can treat, those are the ones that I cure.'

'Oh, really?'

'Yes. That is why I do well. Tantric healing works where other treatments don't!'

'Have you cured any illnesses through these means?'

'What strange things you say, brother! I've cured the toughest of maladies with these methods.'

'Oh, I see!'

'I know you are educated in English and in the modern sciences, and don't trust these alternative treatments that I offer. But do you believe in ghosts?'

Good God, I thought. From Tantric treatments he is now moving on to ghosts and goblins! It looks like Kashi Kobiraj knows many things indeed!

'And what if I say I don't?' I responded.

'Of course, that is what you will say. Your past has been wasted in these modern thoughts and ideas, and that is what will take up your future as well! Don't be angry, brother. I only said what is true. Ah, the tea has arrived. Then listen to a story about something I have seen with my own eyes.'

By now the rain was pelting down and it had become quite dark as well. Kashi started narrating his story.

Kashi Kobiraj is known for his alternative methods of treatment and people from near and far call on him for his services. Around ten years back he was called upon to treat the son of Hariharpur's *zamindar*, Shibchandra Mukherjee.

I asked, 'Had you ever been to his house before?'

'No.'

'Had you heard of him?'

'A lot. In those parts, the name of Hariharpur's zamindar was quite well known.'

'What time of day was it when you reached his house?'

'Just before dusk. And now listen to my story.'

At the sight of the house, Kashinath was filled with wonder. The zamindar's house was imposing. It stood two or three storeys tall and had a huge porch. Close to the porch, there was a sitting room, and adjoining it was a large verandah. On the other side were the worship hall and a hall for staging village theatre. But most of it was in a dilapidated condition—still standing tall, but only as a reminder of the grandeur and prosperity that once was. Banyan and peepal trees had taken root in its ancient walls. At the outer edge of the verandah stood a temple. The crown of the temple had cracked in several places through the passage of time, and its crevices now housed nesting-holes of jungle mynas and squirrels. Opposite the temple was a pond, only half-paved and covered with water hyacinth.

Standing there and looking at that ancient, broken-down manor house, with dusk about to fall, Kashinath felt a strange sensation.

'Strange? How do you mean?'

'That is difficult to explain, brother. It was neither fear nor elation. I felt as if this was an ill-omened house and that it would be inadvisable for me to step within its walls. You may not have felt that way had you been there, but that is how I felt.'

'Have you ever felt that way at any other place you've visited?'

'Yes, once or twice. But let's not go into that now.'

Kashinath then went inside and examined the patient—a ten-year-old boy, suffering from a high fever brought on by typhoid.

The child was already in a bad state. Kashinath employed his Tantric practices on him. He also prepared some native medicinal concoctions derived from herbs and roots and administered them to the boy. The patient subsequently seemed to revive and improve somewhat.

Late in the night, having had his meal, Kashi entered the sitting room next to the courtyard and saw that his bed had already been made. A very fine bedstead it was, with a mosquito net of expensive netting. There was water in a covered brass tumbler and *paan* in a fine box—the arrangements all immaculate and tidy.

I said, 'That must have been so...since the family had such a name.'

'Yes, quite an aristocratic family it was always known to have been!' Kashi responded. 'Even if they had come upon bad times, old habits and ways of living die hard.'

'What happened next?' I asked.

Kashinath hadn't been in bed for very long, when he observed a veiled woman coming towards the house from somewhere in the direction of the grounds. Walking swiftly, she entered the courtyard and went into the house. Kashi was taken by surprise. Who could possibly come from the grounds and enter the house so late in the night? From what he could make out, the lady seemed to be beautiful and of fine figure, and from a good family.

Anyway, he had come to the house in his capacity as a village physician. He only needed to provide his services here. Why should he concern himself with the internal matters of the family?

I asked him, 'What time of the night was it when this happened?'

'About one o'clock. Could have been later.'

'The direction from which you saw her coming...were there any lights? Any signs of human habitation?'

'None at all—just empty lands and after that a river. There is no water in that river during the summers—one can walk across it. And beyond that lies Balrampur village.'

'How could you make out that the woman was of a good and noble family?'

'She was extremely fair of complexion and noble of bearing. This I could clearly make out in the light of the half-moon, although her face was veiled and couldn't be seen.'

'While she was entering the house, did you observe anyone else there?'

'No.'

'Do you think she noticed your presence?'

'No, she was looking straight ahead and went directly into the house.'

Kashinath, undoubtedly a simple and good-hearted fellow, drank some water, adjusted the mosquito net and lay down to sleep. But various thoughts were going around in his head and he was unable to find slumber. He kept tossing and turning on the bed. People don't invite physicians into their house for them to fall into a senseless sleep. Kashinath is a man of experience, with a sufficiently strong sense of responsibility, and having come to cure a patient in the house, how could he possibly allow himself to fall asleep so carelessly?

After a minute or two, Kashinath suddenly observed that the woman, who had gone into the house a while ago, had emerged again and was making her way past the porch. Kashinath almost jumped out of bed in surprise. The woman swiftly walked towards the empty fields and continued beyond. Even as she went further away, Kashinath could still clearly make out her white clothes in the half-moon-lit night.

I asked, 'She went all alone towards those empty fields?'

'Yes, indeed. And that too in the deep of night.'

'What were your thoughts at that time?'

'What sense could I possibly make of it? I was quite taken by surprise! I could never have imagined that a beautiful woman could possibly make her way all alone, so late at night, through such remote and solitary paths.'

Kashinath was trying to calm his senses, when a servant rushed out of the house to tell him, 'Make haste, sir! The patient seems to be in a bad state.'

Kashinath went to the boy and saw that the child's condition had indeed taken a turn for the worse. But he hadn't expected it to deteriorate so suddenly. Kashinath administered whatever suitable medications he could to improve his patient's condition, and after some effort, the boy's condition became a little stable. Kashinath went back and lay down in his bedroom adjacent to the courtyard.

The next day saw the boy's condition improving. Zamindar Sahib, the boy's father, had been in very low spirits on the first day when the physician had met him, but observing some improvement in his son's health, he now felt a sense of relief—so much so that he even played a game of dice with Kashi. He also invited him to go fishing in their large family pond. Special arrangements were made for lunch that day with delicacies like carp head, sweetened curd, milk and *sandesh*, among other dishes. Kashi was quite happy, and Zamindar *Babu* was also content.

Another strange incident occurred that night—something beyond Kashi's wildest imagination. After an early dinner, he took himself to bed, but couldn't fall asleep for a long time. Somewhere, he heard a clock strike one. At that same moment, Kashi saw the veiled woman of the previous night again entering the courtyard and making her way towards the house.

Needless to say, Kashi was amazed. Quite a braveheart this woman was! Walking through those empty fields all alone in the middle of the night. Didn't she have any fear whatsoever?

About fifteen minutes went by—and such long minutes they seemed to be! Next thing he knew, the woman had suddenly entered Kashinath's room!

'In your room, did you say?' I asked.

'Yes indeed. Right in front of me.'

'Was there light in the room?'

'On account of there being a patient in the house, a hurricane lamp was always kept alight in my room through the night.'

On entering the room, the woman lifted her veil slightly and looked at Kashi. A very beautiful lady she was, with a face that inspired awe and reverence. Addressing the physician, she said, 'Don't stay here anymore. Leave this place at once.'

Wide-eyed and stupefied, Kashi looked at the lady and asked, 'Who are you, *Ma*?'

'Whoever I may be, will you leave this place or not is what I wish to know.'

'Ma, I'm a physician. I have come here to treat a patient. How can I leave this place before I fulfil my duties?'

'You won't be able to save this patient. Tomorrow morning you must leave this place.'

'How do you know that the patient won't survive?' Kashi asked, puzzled.

'I am the boy's mother. His stepmother is causing him a lot of anguish; my little boy is going through such agony. I cannot bear it. I've come to take him away with me—and take him away I must. You won't be able to hold onto him for long now...'

Even then Kashi couldn't quite understand what the lady was implying. He somehow managed to ask, 'Where do you stay, my lady?'

'It's been four years since I died. The boy's father has married again now. The stepmother is torturing my son. I cannot let this be. I cannot be at peace. My little boy suffers and cries alone—I hear him. I must take him away with me. Why do you want your practice to earn a bad name? Be on your way. Go back to where you belong.'

Kashinath felt his entire body go cold. He had hardly had time to understand what had just taken place. It still hadn't sunk in. Even so, he said with folded hands, 'Ma, there's something I wish to say. Let me inform your husband, the Zamindar Babu about the situation. He loves his son deeply. You must consider what grief he will come to should you take the boy away.'

'He will beget children through his second wife. He will be able to spend his life with them,' the lady replied.

'Please don't say that, Ma. If you don't think about his well-being, who else will? Please consider the matter from all perspectives. You must think about him too. I will myself go and tell him everything clearly. If he is willing to have a talk with his present wife and prevent any further torment to his son, then will you give me your word that you won't take the boy with you? Will you allow me to make this effort, Ma?'

'All right,' the lady replied.

After saying this, the lady did not disappear instantly, however. She left the room, exited the porch and making her way towards the fields, mingled into the mist of the hoary night.

I exclaimed, 'What the deuce!'

'Oh yes,' Kashinath said.

'Tell me, wasn't the figure of the lady vague and hazy in parts at least?'

'No, exactly as you would expect a human figure to be. Nothing indistinct or shadowy. I conversed with her as well. I didn't feel any terror. I felt as if I was speaking with a noble lady of a good house.'

Sometime after this, a servant came from inside the house to call Kashi. The patient's health had taken a turn for the worse. And yet, he had been quite all right through the day. The physician treated him with whatever remedies he could, and before dawn sought out the zamindar and said to him, 'There's something I need to talk to you about. Please let's go outside.'

I said, 'So did you tell him everything?'

'Yes, right from the very beginning. I said to him: "Where you are standing now—only a while ago, your first wife was standing at this very spot."'

'Did he believe you?' I ventured to ask.

'He broke down and said, "I know...After my boy fell ill, I saw her in his room once, standing next to his bed and looking at him transfixed!"'

The story after that is quite brief, really.

Zamindar Babu said, 'I am aware that the boy's stepmother has not been too kind to him, but I had no idea that things were this bad. I give my word—if and when the boy recovers, I'll have him sent to his maternal uncle's place, and arrange for him to be educated there. I won't let him go through this again. I'll also give strict instructions to my present wife. Please convey this to my first wife.'

Morning dawned.

The patient gradually started improving. Eleven days later, Kashinath confirmed that the boy was out of danger.

I asked, 'Didn't you see the boy's mother again? Did she come to meet you?'

'No,' the physician replied.

Previously published in Bengali as '*Kashi Kobirajer Golpo*' in *Bibhutibhushan Golpo Shomogro*.

A Day

I was feeling quite low. Sometimes there are days like this. One doesn't feel like reading anything or thinking about anything. You don't even feel like talking to anybody. It feels as if the wheel of your mind has run out of oil, and unless you apply oil to the wheel it won't work well anymore. It will gradually fall to rust and, one day, suddenly stop working altogether.

I took myself to an old card house at Jele Para Lane. All the old friends have come and gathered there, but cards don't appeal to me this evening. On other days, I would feel so happy and excited at the thought of playing cards and winning. But today I feel even if I end up winning, what's the big deal? The gossip floating around didn't appeal to me either. Absolutely meaningless was that low sitting room, meaningless the sand and lime-washed walls, the same boring, cheap oleographs hanging on them—*The Destruction of Demon Kalia*, *Annapurna's Charity*, some silly landscape—and the same boring, everyday conversations that I'd been hearing for eternity. Suddenly I felt insipid and ill-disposed towards everything. It all seemed frivolous and so pointless. I asked the man next to me, 'Do you feel happy here? Doesn't this place bother you?'

He gave me a long look, a curious and surprised expression on his face, and said, 'Why? Why wouldn't I feel happy out here! Why do you ask?'

I began to feel bitter and resentful, and this feeling went from bad to worse until finally, I left the place on the pretext of some work. It was four in the evening. Peddlers were going about their work in the streets, calling out loudly to advertise their wares. Boys, carrying bags on their shoulders, were returning from school. The sound of water falling from taps was coming from somewhere nearby, and in the meantime, small groups of gossip-mongers had taken their place at every turn of the street.

I was passing through an extremely narrow, dark alley. I often pass through this street. There is a municipal bathing place close by, and near it stands a tin-roofed room. This room and its inhabitants are, for me, objects of intense curiosity. A small room, five-by-five at the most—that is all there is to it. Within this constricted space stays a family—a husband-wife and their two small children. Unless one sees it, it is difficult to believe how these many people could stay in such a small, restricted place, along with their belongings. Even more surprising is the fact that in a corner of that five-by-five room is their kitchen! Whenever I pass through that way, I find something or the other cooking on the stove—the woman of the house, clutching her baby close to her, busy preparing something or maybe simply warming the milk. Looking at her it's difficult to make out her age—she could be twenty-three, or maybe thirty, or even forty. Her veil is torn, a long-used, dirty sari adorns her figure, a coloured bangle or two graces her wrists. A dull-looking face, seemingly devoid of any good sense. Her husband probably works as a labourer or artisan in some factory; on some evenings, while on my way back, I have seen him—dirt-marked face and clothes, a small bucket in his hand, making his way to the nearby municipal bathing house.

Today also I saw them. The woman was sitting near the doorstep, her baby boy in her lap, lavishing her motherly love on him. She looked at me with a stupid expression as I passed by. The same tiny room, almost like a pigeon hole, the walls layered with mud, a layer of newspapers covering them, yellowed and faded with the passage of time, some dirty clothes hanging on the washing line.

All this made me feel worse. How do they manage to derive joy from such conditions? How do they continue to be? Such a worthless existence! Why do they keep going on? And what would that baby boy grow up to be? The same kind of labourer that his father is today; he too would live in the same kind of makeshift house with his wife and children, the same dirty, ugly, dark and meaningless existence, living out his days one by one, moving inexorably towards an unremarkable death! And yet, with what eagerness and enthusiasm is the mother grasping the infant close to her chest and showering him with love! Possibly with innumerable hopes and sweet dreams of their future. But even this thought gave way to doubt. Does she even have the intelligence to dream of a particular future? Does she have the imagination to think of herself in a situation that doesn't currently exist, but could become possible in the future if she so wished? Can she form a distinct shape in her mind of her hopes and desires? Can she shake off the reality of her narrow, ugly existence in the hope of a finer, brighter future?

Reaching the main road, I went winding through the book stalls that lined its turnings. Loads and loads of old books and magazines, most of them cheap. Creations of an idle, immature mind. Foreign novels with shiny covers and movie magazines, among others. On other days, I search through the piles, just in case I find something useful. But today I didn't have the patience to sort through the mess. The mind's sky today felt like a faded coin, having neither the brilliance of a bright blue sky nor the dull, natural beauty of a cloudy day—indeed just like a faded coin.

Should I go to the cinema? Or should I go for a walk towards Outram Ghats? Should I sit somewhere and have hot tea? Go towards the lake, maybe?

A crowd had gathered in front of the church at Dharmatala. A man wearing English clothes was lying unconscious on the footpath, the head and the body forming such a strange angle with each other that it looked as if he was dead. Two sergeants arrived. People said he had been found lying unconscious inside the ground-floor bathroom of the opposite house. The guard of the house had informed other people and together they had helped bring the man out and laid him down on the footpath. They didn't know who the man was. He was not dead but simply unconscious under the influence of excessive alcohol. The sergeants had the unresponsive body loaded into a taxi and then took him away.

I felt sympathy for the man. The sympathy which I hadn't felt for that ignorant woman in the dark alley was now aroused at the sight of this unconscious drunkard. The poor man had ventured out looking for joy, had even determined on a path to take, possibly the wrong path, possibly the honest one. It is the honesty of the search for happiness which ought to be its yardstick. Who can say what the man's experience in life was, what for him was the value of that search for happiness? The one who knew, who could answer, was unconscious and senseless.

I reached Curzon Park. Several servants and ayahs, together with the small children of English sahibs who had ventured out under their care, had taken shelter under the awnings that covered the footpath benches, clearly wanting to take refuge from the impending rain. The rain was now gradually increasing in intensity. I too went and stood with them. A toddler—curly golden hair, blue eyes, possibly a year and half old or two—picked up his boy-servant's cap from the ground, and floundering slightly, stretched out with the utmost effort, and somehow managed to place it back on the servant's head. Once done, he seemed to find in it an immense satisfaction and swinging his little arms and dancing, broke into a toothless giggle of uncontrollable mirth. But he hasn't been able to place the cap properly on its owner's head, for within a moment or two it rolls over and falls back to the ground; yet again the child picks it up and with renewed effort tries to place it back where it rightfully belongs—and again the same laughter, the same joyful swinging of arms and legs, the same little jig. Nobody is observing him, nor does he expect anyone to pay attention to his play; his boy-servant has so lost himself in an intimate conversation with the ayah sitting next to him that he has no awareness whatsoever of what the toddler is engaged in. The other children in the group are all too small to take any notice. The little boy is busy in his play—fetching the cap from the ground and depositing it on the servant's head, time and again.

Spellbound, I keep gazing at him, observing his activity. The fascinating rhythm of those soft hands and feet, what expressive liveliness, what innocent cheer, what glorious beauty! Over and over again he flops down joyfully on the ground with a rush to fetch the cap, laughing loudly, now raising his little fists, now bringing them down again—what a fascinating, wordless, undisguised expression of infantine zeal! I am unable to take my eyes off him. As if predestined, I'd suddenly been brought and thrown in front of unanticipated beauty. I kept standing there for a long time. The servant suddenly seemed to come back to his senses. Interrupting his conversation with the ayah for a moment and turning to the child, he snatches the cap from the boy's hand and deposits it inside a perambulator. The child's face darkens; wobbling on his little feet he takes himself to the perambulator, but it is too high for him—his little hands cannot reach inside it. He looks around helplessly at first, and then slumps down to sit on the ground—the servant oblivious to it all, is again lost in conversation with the ayah.

I walked into Curzon Park and sat on a bench. The sun was about to set, the sky over the opposite bank of the Ganges all red and full of colour.

The meaningless joy of the child's heart had unknowingly infected me as well. The woman of the tin-roofed house somehow didn't seem so ignorant anymore.

Previously published in Bengali as '*Aekti Din*' in *Bibhutibhushan Golpo Shomogro*.

The Tiger Mantra

It was quite chilly outside that day. Sitting together in the *Rai Bahadur*'s drawing-room, conversation was in full flow. There were quite a lot of us that day. With the arrival of piping hot tea and a snack of puffed rice, the gathering had become very lively indeed.

The Rai Bahadur is a gracious friend and a very well-known *shikari*. Who amongst us isn't aware of his fame and eminence? When you enter his house, you can see busts of tigers all around you and several bear skins sprawled on the floors. In every room you enter, animal heads look down at you from the walls. It makes you feel as if you have stepped into a taxidermist's workshop!

But that day, I saw a tall, elderly person sitting next to the Rai Bahadur and talking of things related to *shikar*. I was quite mystified, because I haven't yet come across anyone who knows more about shikar than the Rai Bahadur. In his lifetime, the Rai Bahadur has hunted thirty Royal Bengal tigers, fifteen leopards, countless bears and wild boars, not to mention rhinos, bison, pythons, porcupines, egrets and ducks. To sit next to such a man and talk about hunting! Who could this person be? I was most curious to know his identity.

Upen *Babu*, our very own Upen Maiti, was sitting next to me, drinking one cup of tea after another. I turned to him and asked, 'Upen Babu, who is that gentleman?'

As if taken by surprise, Upen Babu said, 'What did you say? Who? Where?'

'Don't be so startled. I only asked who that person is.'

'*Him*, you mean?'

'Yes. Tell me who he is.'

'Former shikari, Nidhiram Bhattacharya.'

'The name sounds like that of some judicial expert. You could just as easily say Justice Nidhiram Bhattacharya.'

'Well, he is not exactly a non-entity in matters of hunting. Haven't you read his book, *An Occasion for Shikar*? The book has already seen three editions. Come, I will introduce you to him.'

I was introduced to the man. Although he was a Brahmin, the fact that he hadn't spent his life working as a priest had become readily evident when I'd first heard his manner of speech, and when I spoke to him, it became clearer still. He talked about how tigers and bears are hunted in various parts of the country; how he had to spend nights on tree tops waiting for the object of his hunt; how in some jungle he had once almost become a meal for a tiger, and other such stories. The man had a talent for story-telling. He narrated the stories so beautifully that we could almost see the events unfolding in front of our very eyes! Another thing I noted was that he was a true nature lover. Sitting there in the drawing-room, he gave such a marvellous description of moonlit, rainy *Shravan* nights!

I ventured to say, 'Tell us about an extraordinary experience that you've had.'

Nidhiram Bhattacharya said, 'Everything about the jungle is extraordinary. Everything is wondrous and amazing.'

'Even so,' I said.

'Even so what? You want a supernatural story? I've never seen a ghost with my own eyes.'

'But do you believe they exist?'

'No,' he replied.

What a strange man! I have never come across a Bengali who doesn't believe in ghosts. Later, however, from his expressions and the substance of his speech, I realised that he believed in *tantra-mantra*.

'Doesn't your *Tantra shastra* believe in spirits?' I asked.

'I haven't studied Tantra shastra. I'm only referring to tantra-mantra.'

'Oh! What kind of tantra-mantra?'

'Never mind. It's all nonsense, fallacious nonsense.

'All nonsense?'

'Entirely.'

'I cannot go so far as to say that there is no substance to it. Surely there is some kind of power in mantras,' I ventured.

'It is precisely this attitude that has ruined the country,' he said sharply. 'In spite of being educated in the modern sciences, you believe in all this?'

My respect for the man was immediately awakened. An elderly person, with a modern and progressive outlook. Quite an amazing fellow!

I asked, 'Have you been to the Sundarbans?'

'Many a time. Let me narrate to you an incident that took place there, related to this tantra-mantra that you speak of.'

All ears, I went up and sat close to him. The day was certainly appropriate for listening to such stories.

'At the time that I speak of,' he began, 'our barge was positioned at Kakdangar tank. Our guru on shikar-related matters, Shyamacharan Ray, the nephew of Advocate Sitakant Ray of Khulna, was with us. I should have said this the other way round. Actually, we were with him—else, how could people of our status and position possibly arrange for a barge?

'The place where the barge was tied was close to the mouth of a creek. Passing through dense forests the Kakdangar creek had joined the river at this point. The creek presented a beautiful sight. On either side, there were dense thickets of *hetal*, and in the midst of the jungle there were *goran* and *golpata* trees. The edge of the water was lined with tiger ferns. It is in the dense undergrowth formed by these ferns that the enormous tigers of the Sundarbans normally hide. Shyamacharan Ray took a pinch of tobacco and said, "Put the cockleboat towards the Kakdangar creek."

'Seated in the boat, we made our way into the creek. Those who have not been to the Sundarbans cannot understand the wonder and beauty that meets the eye when you pass through the jungle in a boat—thick undergrowth in some places and wild lemon trees in another, rows of palm trees and at some places, an abundance of pomelo or other fruits. At some point, one might see that a burst of yellow flowers has lit up the creepers, or that *keya* flowers blooming in dense shrubs have invigorated the forest air with a sweet smell.

'Many people say that the Sundarbans is humdrum and monotonous. Such people have never seen this forest on a moonlit night. Nor have they seen its beauty just before dawn, when the silent jungle is enveloped in colours of multiple hues. They haven't heard its diverse sounds or the cries and calls of the birds that inhabit it. My guru Shyamacharan Ray was so much in love with these jungles that he'd told his family that when he died his body must be buried in the Sundarbans. His soul would thereby rest in peace.'

I asked, 'Is he still alive?'

'No,' replied Nidhiram Babu. 'It has been many years since he passed away.'

'Was his body buried in the midst of the forest?'

'No. A Hindu's body is not supposed to be buried; society would object. So it wasn't done.'

'That is really sad. But please go on with your story.'

'Then listen. But there's one thing I have to say—until I'm finished with the story, you must not protest or object to anything that I say.'

'Fine, please go ahead.'

Nidhiram Babu took a long drag on his cigarette, recovered his breath, and releasing puffs of smoke into the air, continued his story.

'Floating down the creek, we reached the thick of the jungle. To tell you the truth, more than the addiction of being part of a shikar, it was the sights and sounds of the dense jungle that had taken a hold of me. We had gone more than a mile from the river, when all of a sudden a voice called out from the dense undergrowth that lined the creek, "Babu! O Babu *log*!"

'We were scared out of our wits. Our boatman let out a *Ram-Ram*!

'Shyamacharan Ray looked towards the shore of the creek and, raising his voice, said, "Shut up all of you!"

'"Who's there?" he asked.

'In a feeble voice someone replied, "Babu, it's me."

'"Who are you? And where are you? Come out in the open."

'"I am here, Babu, sitting close to the undergrowth."

'True, all this while, being unable to see the man, we had mistakenly assumed that the voice belonged to some bodiless entity. But then he gradually came into view. There, he was seated to the right of a bush. I realised then that he had been visible before as well. But in the interplay of light and shadows, when viewed over the waters at that distance, he'd looked just like the cropped trunk of a tree. Naturally, we were amazed to see him sitting there all alone. Those who are familiar with the Sundarbans will know that even a daft person would be afraid to remain alone in the middle of the jungle.

'Shyamacharan Ray said, "Okay, fine. But what are you doing sitting there?"

'"Babu, I was eating the fruits of the hetal. I'm very hungry. I am a poor man!"

'"That's not the appropriate answer to my question. Feeling hunger is the law and creed of the body, so that's not what is surprising. It is also true that if one enters this jungle, there is rarely any food to be found other than some ripe fruits. But the point is how did you come to be here?"

'"Babu, I am but a *fakir*. How can I afford to feel fear? Can you please give me a ride on your boat, Babu? If you take me up to the KalRanghat tank, I can walk up to the *pir*'s *dargah* to spend the night there, and leave for my home tomorrow morning. Will you take me along, Babu?"

'"Is that where you live?"

'"My home is in Manik Sen's *para*, close to KalRanghat," said the man.

'Before Shyamacharan Babu could say anything, the two oarsmen of our boat, objecting to the proposal, said, "Don't take him, Babu! You must know the law of the boat. In the Sundarbans, if a man is taken into a running boat, it is considered ill-omened, and extremely so. Since Babu has ventured on an important task..."

'This angered Shyamacharan Babu, and he said, "Really, you fellows have no sense!"

'"Why do you say so, Babu?" asked the oarsmen.

'"Whether I succeed in my shikar or not, how can I leave him here to become a meal for a tiger? Take him along."

'Who could possibly disagree? The boat was stopped and the man allowed to get in. He did appear to be a fakir. Looking at his attire and appearance, that is what I thought to myself then. It was difficult to make out whether he was a Hindu or a Mussalman. However, we didn't say anything. Shyamacharan Babu asked the man, "What do you practise?"

'"I know the mantra to attract and draw a tiger up close. That is my practice."

'"What's that you say?" I asked the man.

'"Indeed, there is such a mantra, Babu. My guru taught it to me."

'Shyamacharan Babu asked, "Do you put your lips to the mouth of a pot and call out to the tiger?"

'"No, Babu. It is the power of the mantra that draws the tiger."

'"We're on our way to a shikar. If you can draw a tiger close enough for us to take a shot at, you will be rewarded with a *baksheesh* of ten rupees."

'"Babu! You are merciful!"

'"But don't try to fool us."

'"You need not even say that, Babu."

'By that time, we had all surrounded the man and were listening to him speak. Shyamacharan Babu said, "There are a few people in the Sundarbans who can bring a tiger right in front of the shikaris, and they earn a bit of money through this. They put their lips to the mouth of an empty pot and call out to the animal. So you don't belong to that group?"

'"It is as I've told you, Babu. The mantra is the real thing. It draws the tiger."'

At this point, we asked Nidhiram Babu, 'What's this you mentioned about putting one's lips to the mouth of a pot and calling out to a tiger?'

Nidhiram Babu explained, 'There is a section of people for whom this is an occupation. They sit in the undergrowth and, applying their lips to the mouth of an empty pot, imitate the call of a tigress. Hearing this call, male tigers rush towards the source of the sound, and fall prey to a shot from the shikari's gun. Before the War, their fee for this service was five rupees. Can't say how much they charge now.'

We asked, 'Have you seen tigers being enticed in this way?'

'Many a time. But their efforts don't always bear fruit. Especially when there are no tigers in that jungle or no tigers close by at that point of time. Or else, sensing the presence of humans, they retreat into the depths of the forest. How could such a technique possibly work then?'

Nidhiram Babu then said, 'Now listen to the rest of the story. I'm a *pukka* shikari, and I had never heard that a mantra could tempt a tiger to come close to you. If this were true, can you imagine how much the practice of shikar could benefit from it? *Moshai*, those who are fond of shikar know how much labour needs to be put into tracking a tiger. You either have to walk for miles through the jungle, or else keep awake all night waiting on a machan. Do you think it is easy? And imagine if a tiger can be drawn by chanting a mantra, how easy the hunt will be! Why would anyone object to paying ten rupees instead of five?'

'That's true,' said someone. 'Please go on.'

Nidhiram Babu continued, 'About two hours went by. Having reached midway into the creek we anchored the boat.

'Dusk was approaching. We didn't dare set foot on the shore at that time of the day. The food for the night had been brought along, and after having our meals, we spent the night resting in the boat. That entire night, Shyamacharan Babu was sleepless with excitement. He spent the night listening to the ludicrous tales of tantra-mantra from the fakir—about how many times he had practised the mantra to attract tigers in these forests, and how sitting in the most remote and densest of these forests and practising the mantra is what occupied much of his time. And more such nonsensical talk! After a long, hard day, one would like to get some rest in the night, but that was not possible.

'Shyamacharan Ray was himself Fakir Sahib's supporter. Who would contradict him? Lying there in the boat, we attempted to sleep, but it was only in the early hours before dawn that we managed to get any.'

I said, 'Just one question. Why did you go halfway up the Kakdangar creek? What was the purpose of leaving the barge behind and going all the way into the middle of the creek?'

'The purpose was very clear,' Nidhiram Babu said. 'You cannot possibly hunt if you are sitting in the barge! The barge is stationed in the river; on one side is the jungle, and on the other, you may or may not get to see the shore. If you don't enter a creek, you won't get to see the jungle on either side. You haven't gone into the jungle for a picnic, have you?'

Nidhiram Bhattacharya is a bit of an argumentative person. He is always alert and sensitive to the possibility of someone questioning him, and should such an eventuality arise, he is always ready to argue. Now I understood why prior to beginning his story he'd asked that no one interrupt or question him during the narration. We somehow managed to appease him, saying, 'We question you from time to time not to find fault with your story but only because we are curious. Please continue.'

Nidhiram Babu said, 'Fine then. Now listen to the rest of it. My story is about to end. All I'm saying is whatever you need to ask, you can do so at the end, once I'm done telling the story.'

He continued, 'After anchoring the boat deep in the jungle and spending the night there, we realised what a formidable and frightening place we had entered. That moonlit night, intermingled with light and shadows, started resounding and shaking with the roar of the tiger. Shyamacharan Ray's judgement regarding the Kakdangar creek hadn't been misplaced. In the morning, I told Shyamacharan Babu, "It's an amazing place you've brought us to!"

'Shyamacharan Ray said, "You speak like an amateur shikari!"

'"Why do you say so?"

'"The tiger of the forest and the tiger of the shikari are not the same. There are innumerable places in the Sundarbans where tigers call out in the way you heard them do last night. But you'll never be able to see even one of them with your eyes. That's why I've caught hold of Fakir Sahib. Now it's all up to him."

'"And the skill of your hands," I said.

'When the morning sun had risen well above the horizon, all of us alighted from the boat and entered the jungle. About a mile from where we started there was a clearing in the forest known as the Hatol Badiyar glade where we would cook our food and have our lunch.

'We took all the things we needed when we left the boat and carried them with us. Who would return to the boat, walking through all that jungle again only to fetch things we needed for cooking? The two boatmen came along too as they were not willing to stay back on the boat in the middle of that lonesome jungle.

'On either side of us were dense jungles of goran and hetal, and a concentration of tiger ferns. One has to watch one's step and keep an eye out for *shulo*. These are the aerial roots of trees rising up from the wetlands. They can be pretty sharp. They stand straight up like spears, often hidden beneath the fallen dry leaves that cover the forest floor. If one were to step on them, it would immediately cause one to bleed. With the jungle flanking us on both sides, we were on the narrow path in between that could be covered on foot.

'The Fakir Sahib was at the very front, immediately behind him was Guruji Shyamacharan Ray, then two other people, followed by me, and the two boatmen at the rear.

'All of a sudden, a sound was heard. Shyamacharan Babu and the two people behind him stopped abruptly in their tracks.

'I asked, "What happened? Why did you stop?" I was a bit distracted and not knowing what the matter was, kept going.

'At that moment I glanced towards the front of our group. Fakir Sahib had been right in the front, but he wasn't there anymore. I was about to say, "Fakir Sahib, I believe..." when Shyamacharan Babu broke in saying, "Oh no! Such a terrible thing to happen...Oh!"

'The two people behind him were standing dumbfounded. One of them said, "Oh! From the bush on Babu's right..."

'Shyamacharan Babu said in a benumbed voice, "Oh! The poor man! I told him to keep chanting the mantra in his head."

'And that's when I heard the entire thing. From the dense thicket of tiger ferns to our right, a massive Royal Bengal tiger had leapt out and carried away the Fakir Sahib. Looking at the hetal bushes on the left, it seemed as if the tops of the bushes were still shaking.'

Giving a long sigh, I said, 'And then? Was Fakir Sahib found?'

'Does that ever happen?' said Nidhiram Babu. 'That was the end of it. Only a *mala* made of Hinglaj beads could be seen hanging from the branch of a hetal bush. We spent a long time looking for him. Shyamacharan Ray was an accomplished shikari. He knew a lot about the ways of the tiger, its habits and propensities, but he couldn't do a thing. We didn't even know Fakir Sahib's name so that we might send the news to his people.

'My guruji Shyamacharan Ray used to say, "The man had the ability. He had indeed been able to draw the tiger with the power of his mantra, but was killed due to my carelessness. He had only learnt the art of attracting a tiger, not the way to save himself from its jaws!"

'After we searched the area where the attack had taken place, we went back up the Kakdangar creek to the barge on the river. Everybody was so distressed and downcast that no one had any enthusiasm for shikar anymore.

'I asked Shyamacharan Babu, "Guruji, who asked Fakir Sahib to be in the lead? You know well that an unarmed person should never lead the group in that manner."

'Shyamacharan Ray replied, "I never trusted him. Like all of you, I too thought his claims were bogus!"'

Previously published in Bengali as '*Bagher Montor*' in *Bibhutibhushan Golpo Shomogro*.

Master Vidhu

I shall never be able to forget Master Vidhu. I shall probably carry the memory of him all my life. He had come into my life only for a few months, and our acquaintance was brief, but the memory of it still lives in me today.

I clearly remember that day. It was early morning on a Sunday. I'd opened my grammar book. With my eyes closed and swaying gently back and forth, I was memorising conjugations, when I heard someone calling outside: 'Is Haran *Babu* in? Haran Babu?'

I looked out of the window and asked, 'Whom do you want?'

'Haran Babu. Does he live here?'

'Yes, he does. He is my uncle.'

'Can you please call him?'

'What do you want with him?' I asked.

'I hear that he is looking for a tutor. Is that true?'

The man was right; my uncle was looking for a tutor for us children and had given an advertisement in the newspaper. I had almost forgotten about it. I asked the gentleman, 'So you've seen the advertisement, and that is why you are here, aren't you?'

'Yes,' he replied.

'Please come inside and sit down, while I call my uncle.'

Long-legged, tall, darkish, and looking extremely uncertain, the man entered our drawing room.

I requested him to be seated. Fearful and hesitant, he sat down on a bench. Looking at this inexperienced and modest man, whatever notions of respect I might have had for a master were put to rest. I invited him to sit on a chair.

He politely refused at first, but finally assented and left the humble bench to sit on one of the chairs. I switched on the fan and went upstairs to call my uncle. Uncle came down the stairs, with me following him, and Jhontu, Montu, Chand and Reba not far behind.

As soon as my uncle entered the sitting room, the gentleman got up from his seat and joined his hands together in greeting. Uncle said, 'So you've come in response to my advertisement in today's morning paper, right?'

The gentleman replied in the affirmative.

Addressing the man again, and indicating us, my uncle told him that he was required to teach all five of us for three hours in the evening. As mentioned in the advertisement, he would be paid a tuition fee of seven rupees for his services, but any absenteeism would be frowned upon.

The man said, 'But why would I absent myself from my duties?'

My uncle asked him where he lived.

'Shrinath Das Lane,' said the man.

'And your name?'

'Shri Vidhubhushan Chattopadhyay.'

'How far have you studied?' my uncle further asked.

'I've passed my Matriculation.'

Uncle didn't seem to take to the response favourably. Biting his lips and thinking, he knocked his knuckles on the table a few times. Then he asked the man, 'Are you sure you'll be able to teach a boy of the fourth standard?'

I was the only one studying in the fourth standard, the eldest of us five. My chest expanded with a sense of pride. I stared unwavering at Master Vidhu, wondering how he would respond. 'Why wouldn't I be able to do so?' he asked in reply.

'Well then,' said my uncle, 'you can start on Monday. You'll need to come here at 6 p.m. every day.' Turning to us, he said, 'He is your new master. Learn from him and apply your mind well when he is teaching.'

On Monday our new tutor arrived sharp at six in the evening. He asked each one of us our names and scrutinised our books one by one, giving special attention and time to our English books. Having taken a look at them he commented, 'Quite demanding it is, your English syllabus.'

I was delighted to hear him say this! I said, 'Besides English, we're also taught physics and chemistry.'

He was taken by surprise, and said, 'Is that so?'

I brought my science books and showed him. He asked, 'How much have you studied?'

'Properties of air, and the barometer,' I replied.

My words seemed to take him aback, but I was feeling quite elated all the while.

He then turned to Reba and asked her, 'What is your name, my little girl?'

Overcome with shyness, Reba bent her head and looked down. Whenever she comes across a new person, this is how she typically reacts. Prodding her, I said encouragingly, 'Tell him your name.'

Master meanwhile started gently running his hands through little Reba's soft, woolly hair.

Hesitantly, Reba finally said, 'Leba.' She can't pronounce the letter 'r'.

Master said, 'Wonderful! A very fine name you have.'

As the days passed, Reba's shyness began to decrease, and Master Vidhu started to develop a special fondness for her. Why only Reba? He actually became fond of all of us. Quite often, while he was teaching, a peddler used to pass through our street, announcing in a sonorous voice the goodies that he had for sale.

Master often bought us these edibles. The first time he received his payment, he treated all of us children to pomegranate-flavoured ice candy. No wonder, the children loved him. The only one who didn't like him was me. Why that was so, I cannot exactly say. Even so, I had to abide by his instructions because such was my uncle's wish. I feared my uncle more than anyone else, even more than I feared my own mother and father. Under the circumstances, as might be expected, I started to keep a lookout for Master's mistakes and indications of any weaknesses, so that I might secure a release from his command.

One day I asked him, 'Sir, in order to measure the height of a mountain, does one need a barometer?'

He enquired in return, 'Is it indeed required? Who said so?'

'My schoolmaster,' I replied.

'Then it must be so. Where in the textbooks is this stated? Tell me.'

'In the science book.'

'Show it to me then,' he said.

Handing over the book to him I said, 'I haven't understood any of it.'

Turning the pages of the book he replied, 'I'll explain it to you.'

But far from explaining it to me, he himself seemed to be struggling to understand the exact import of that English paragraph. After musing over it for a long time, he somehow provided an explanation for what it said. He then asked me, 'Did you understand?'

'No, nothing at all,' I replied.

He said, 'I'm going to take your book back home with me. I will go over it and then explain it to you in detail.'

He took away the book with him and even returned it to me in good time, but he wasn't able to answer my question. When I told my uncle about this, he said, 'Okay, let me see how he teaches.'

Next day onwards, Uncle started sitting down with us for the lessons to take note of how Master Vidhu taught us. Uncle often found fault with Master Vidhu's teaching. As an example, you might find him saying, 'The last two stanzas of *Lucy Gray*—you'll need to explain those in more detail. These words...

"O'er rough and smooth she trips along
And never looks behind;
And sings a solitary song
That whistles in the wind."

'Their implied meaning should also be explained to the children. Do you understand?' he would ask.

The master didn't usually have much to say on such occasions. He had a lot of respect for my uncle, and carried on with his job of teaching us. He wasn't terribly good at solving mathematical problems. One day when he was trying to solve an equation, Uncle said, 'It is all going wrong!'

'How come?' the master asked.

'This is an algebraic problem, and it doesn't look like you'll be able to solve it,' Uncle replied.

In any case, Master Vidhu failed to explain the equation to me. After he had left for the day, my uncle said, 'The master isn't all that useful, is he?'

Soon after, the day of Vishwakarma Puja came around. We children said to Master Vidhu, 'Sir, you'll have to buy us kites and kite-winders.'

He agreed to do so as he had recently received his tuition fee. Master Vidhu took us to a nice shop at the southern end of St. James Square and bought us a whole rupee worth of kites and winders. But he always prohibited us from telling anybody about the things he bought us. He used to give us our gifts in utmost secrecy. On Reba's birthday, he had bought her a mechanised toy train worth three rupees. He had said, 'Don't tell anybody anything about it.'

Three or four days after Vishwakarma Puja, I happened to meet Master Vidhu in Shreenath Das Lane. I greeted him. He saw me and said, 'Hey, Pintu! Where are you off to?'

In reply, I asked, 'Where do you stay, Sir?'

'Quite close by,' he said.

'Do let me visit your place, won't you?' I said.

I was not sure why, but a sudden curiosity to see Master's house overcame me. He hesitated a bit and then showed me the way to his beautiful abode!

He stayed in a small room on top of a ramshackle house. A narrow, rickety and uncertain staircase led to his room. It was so shaky that one almost feared to take it! The small verandah underneath seemed to tremble with the weight of a human being climbing the stairs. Slowly and carefully, I ascended the stairs behind the master. He opened the lock to his door. The room was dirty and miserable looking. The walls had several calendars on them. Swami Vivekanand's photograph was put up on one side. A single cot was propped up on the floor, with a blackened pillow on it, greasy with oil. Master Vidhu asked me to sit down, said, 'I'll be back,' and left the room. I walked around, observing his room. Looking at his meagre, painful existence, my heart sank. There was not another pair of clothes in the room. The one that adorned his person was time-worn and darkened through long usage. He had to make do with just a single pair of clothes. I couldn't help feeling sympathy for him and his condition. I seemed to have forgotten that I quite hated the master. It was as if a change had suddenly come over me.

Soon after, Master Vidhu entered the room, bringing with him some cool refreshments. In perturbation, I let out, 'There was no need for this, Sir!'

He seemed taken by surprise at my words and attitude.

I felt that taking from his hard-earned resources in this manner was like drawing the very blood from his body, drop by drop. Protesting passionately, I said that I wouldn't allow it!

Seeing my willful resistance, the ever-present cheerful smile on his face suddenly faded away, and with a sad and pained expression, he said, 'What is this you're saying, Pintu?'

I couldn't find the heart to say anything else. On my way back home that day I promised myself that I would do something to ensure that hereafter, Master Vidhu didn't spend anything from his tuition fees on us children. The poor fellow was somehow able to maintain his frugal existence in the city with the meagre income from his teaching.

But before my pledge could take shape into action, an unpleasant incident occurred. Uncle took a look at my translation notebook one day, and said to Master Vidhu, 'What are you teaching the children, Master? I see that you know no English at all. What was so wrong with the sentence "I live in a boarding house" that you replaced "in" with "at"? Actually, you failed to catch the mistake! And in the sentence "Every bush and every tree was in bud", in keeping with what rules of grammar did you replace "was" with "were"? How can you possibly teach a boy of the fourth standard?'

Shamefaced, Master Vidhu lowered his gaze. And I? I sensed that some very big trouble was in the offing. Uncle said, 'No wonder the boys are doing badly. Pintu, go and fetch your half-yearly report card.'

Fearful, I brought my progress report and handed it over. Uncle said, 'Take a look! Such poor performance! He has failed in English and has managed to pass the rest of the subjects with the slimmest of margins. Seeing this, I'm afraid I can't possibly continue with you anymore. If I do, it will be like bringing down an axe on the legs of these children. We will look out for another tuition master instead. Come on the second of next month and collect the fees due to you.'

Master Vidhu didn't protest or put up any defence whatsoever. Silent and speechless, he left the house and went away. I couldn't find the courage to look at his face. After all, it was I who was responsible for what had happened. Wasn't it I who time and again went to tell Uncle about Master Vidhu's mistakes—so much so that Uncle's heart and mind gradually became alienated from our teacher?

My head hung low, I kept sitting there like a wrongdoer.

Previously published in Bengali as '*Bidhu Master*' in *Bibhutibhushan Golpo Shomogro*.

The Medal

This incident occurred a few years back, because of which I sometimes tend to feel as if it never really happened. It may have been during a bout of illness and possibly caused by a delusion (or something of that sort) I might have had then that I saw things that didn't actually take place. But when I give it some thought, my heart and mind tell me that that is not how it was, that there is actually no good reason to consider the incident as insignificant, false or unreal, and that my experience of that time and the way I perceived it is the real truth.

It is essential that I narrate the incident in its entirety. In this context, I should state at the very outset that for the past ten years I've had no ill-health of any kind whatsoever. My mind is healthy, and I have no psychological maladies. Moreover, the incident that I'm about to relate took place around four years back, and during that period as well I was completely fine. Throughout my entire stint as a school teacher, I don't recall having encountered anything unbelievable or out-of-the-ordinary. Like most school masters, my everyday routine was extremely simple and rather banal, revolving around the same responsibilities day after day. I've been going through life in the same manner for many years now.

The year that I'm about to speak of—this happened that particular year during the monsoons, sometime after the summer holidays had ended. I was teaching in class one day, when my attention was drawn to two boys engaged in fisticuffs with one another. One of them was trying to forcibly snatch away something from the other. When I scolded them for their undesirable conduct, another pupil cried out, 'Sir! Kamikkhe is trying to snatch Sudhir's medal.'

'Whose medal? What medal are you talking of?' I asked.

The boy named Sudhir stood up from his chair and said, 'My medal, Sir!'

Looking intently at the other boy, I asked, 'Were you trying to take his medal, Kamikkhe?'

Kamikkhe (short for Kamakhyacharan Moulik) said, 'I wasn't trying to take it away, Sir. I just wanted to take a look at it, but he was refusing to show it to me.'

'If he is unwilling to show you his medal, what right do you have to snatch it from him? Sit down! Don't dare act like that again!' I said sternly.

I then gave the students a long speech on the importance of brotherhood and honest dealings. Then I glanced at Sudhir and with some curiosity asked him, 'What medal are they talking about? Where did you find it? Come, let me have a look.'

I'd imagined that in one of the many competitions that are commonly organised in the various *paras* of Calcutta—badminton, swimming, running, and other such activities—Sudhir had come in fourth or attained some similar success and been awarded a medal of the kind that is usually given, and it was quite natural and understandable that he had felt like bringing it to class and showing it with pride to his classmates. It was even possible that using this achievement as a pretext, he would gather the other pupils in the class and go to the headmaster to try and secure leave for everyone for the rest of the session that day. Therefore, when the medal reached my hands, I received it with a contemptuous glance. But one look at the medal, and I sat up straight. This wasn't some cheap medal given away at some *para*-level badminton competition—it was quite old, large, and wonderfully moulded! But what exactly was it?

There was some kind of script on the medal, but in that half-lit classroom I could not clearly make out the words. I turned it around to look at the other side and found an image of a young Queen Victoria engraved on it. I couldn't find my glasses in my pocket and realised that I'd probably left them in the school office. In the meantime, a group of boys had crowded around my desk to have a look at the medal. I admonished them saying, 'Go on! Return to your seats! Don't crowd around here.'

I turned to one of the boys and said, 'Read what is written on the medal.'

With much trouble and at a slow pace—he was only a Class 4 student after all—he somehow managed to read, 'Crimea, Sevastopol...Victoria Regina...'

'And on the other side?' I asked.

'Sergeant S. B. Parkins, Sixth Dragon Guards, the year 1854...'

I was taken aback. This medal was awarded by England's military bureau to Sergeant Parkins of the Dragon Guards for an act of bravery in the battlefield of Sevastopol during the Crimean War. It was definitely no ordinary medal!

Crimea...Sevastopol?...The Charge of the Light Brigade! But how did this medal land up in the hands of Sudhir Saha, an inhabitant of Calcutta's Neelmoni Das Lane?

'Come here,' I said, calling out to Sudhir. 'Where did you get this medal from?'

'It is mine, Sir!' the boy replied.

'I understand it is yours. The question is, where did you find it?'

'My *Dadu* gave it to me, Sir.'

'Any idea where your Dadu got it from?'

'Yes, Sir. A sahib gave it to my Dadu's father for safekeeping.'

'Oh! How's that?'

'Actually, we used to own a wine shop. On one occasion, the sahib had been unable to pay for his drinks, so he gave this medal to Dadu's father in lieu of payment, and never returned to claim it. I heard this from my Dadu.'

I did some calculations and it emerged that eighty-six years had gone by since the medal was issued to Sergeant Parkins (whoever he might have been). Even if one assumed that the gentleman was around twenty years old then, he would be at least a hundred and six now. This meant that he must have died and left for the realms of the dead long since.

It was a Saturday. The school was scheduled to close early. I'd already planned to leave for my ancestral village that day, which I hadn't visited for a long time. A *jaetha-moshai* of mine, who is much interested in history and is quite knowledgeable about it, stays there. I thought if I showed him the medal, he'll be mighty pleased. So I borrowed the medal from Sudhir, telling him that I would return it on the following Monday.

After the school closed for the day, I made my way home and, collecting my suitcase, reached Sealdah station, in time to catch the 2:30 train. By the time I got down at the station in my village, it was already 5:30 in the evening. From the station it was a two-mile walk to my home in the village. Dusk had fallen by the time I reached. I could have got there before dusk, but I hadn't bothered to keep up a swift pace.

It was almost the end of the month of *Bhadra*, and there hadn't been as much rain as one would normally expect. So the pathways and *ghat*s were somewhat dry. Yet, the trees that lined the route already presented a lush greenery that was very soothing to my eyes after my long stay in Calcutta. I preferred therefore to stroll along instead of walking fast. I should mention here that there is no one staying in my ancestral home. For a long time now, an elderly lady in my neighbourhood has been taking care of my meals whenever I stay in the village.

I heard from my aunt that about two weeks back, a childhood friend of mine, Vrindavan, had arrived at the village. Vrindavan had been living abroad for many years. The news that he was back made me extremely happy, and I decided to meet him in the evening. So after having my tea, I left home to take a leisurely walk by the river. Before leaving, I opened my suitcase and put the medal in my pocket, so that I could show it to Vrindavan.

When I reached the river, I saw that because of the rains, the water level had risen considerably and was overflowing the banks on either side. I sat close to the river bank for a long time as dusk gradually began to fall. A colony of bats was returning home for the night. There was not a soul to be seen. The rush of the monsoon water had caused the river to breach its banks at one spot. I thought

I would take a look to see how the breach had come about. The embankment was quite high at the point where I stood, and down below I could see the river, swollen with monsoon water, the rapid current rushing towards its destination. Standing on the edge of the rise, I looked down at the vortex of water below when suddenly, I felt a strange wish take shape in my heart—I would leap from the embankment into that whirl of rushing water! As I continued to stand there, this wish grew stronger with each passing moment. Let me jump! Shall I? And yet, I knew that the swirling river currents were strong, and that if a twig were thrown in, it would be snapped in two. I cannot swim, and the water was deep. But the longer I stood there, the more difficult it became to resist the temptation to jump! I felt I simply must, I have to...or else I would never be happy again.

I could feel my legs growing incredibly heavy. I knew that if I stayed there any longer, I would become altogether incapable of leaving the spot. Somehow, I pulled myself away from that perilous embankment.

Once I left the river bank, however, and made my way towards Vrindavan's house, all traces of that suicidal urge disappeared. I was shocked at the workings of my own mind. How strange! What could it all possibly mean? I recalled that I'd smoked quite a bit during my journey on the train. In the stifling heat of Bhadra, it hadn't been wise to smoke so much. Moreover, I had also drunk two or three cups of tea after reaching home. This might have triggered the strange workings of my mind. Yes, that must have been it.

I walked on to Vrindavan's house. It was indeed very pleasant to meet Vrindavan after all this time. The two of us sat talking late into the night about all that had happened during the many years since we had last met. There was so much to talk about. It was a very hot day, with the typical sultry heat of the month of Bhadra. There was no movement of air whatsoever.

Vrindavan said, 'Come, brother, let's go to the roof and continue our chat. At least, we will find some relief from this heat. You'll have to have dinner at our place today—Ma has said so—and we have already sent a message to that effect to your home.'

The two of us made our way up to the roof. The house was a two-storey building. On the roof of the second floor was a lone room. I knew that Vrindavan's *kaka* stayed in that room. When we got to the roof, I saw that bamboo poles were tied together into a structure at the back of the house. I asked Vrindavan, 'Is there some construction going on in the house?'

'Yes brother, Kaka's room needs repair. From the north-facing wall, the efflorescent bricks are being removed.'

Vrindavan walked into the room on the roof. I followed him. But my mind felt strangely restless. After sitting together and chatting for some time, I felt thirsty and asked for some water. Vrindavan went downstairs to fetch some while I took a stroll on the roof. There was no one else on the roof and it was quite dark out there. I strolled towards the point on the north-facing side where the masons had tied poles for the construction work, and was looking down when I suddenly thought, 'Why not jump from the roof?'

'It would be great! Shall I jump?' The desire to leap off the roof was almost irrepressible. The thought reverberated in my head: 'I want to jump from the roof...I must...Shall I?'

At that moment Vrindavan returned to the roof and said, 'Come into the room. Ma is about to send some tea. Why are you standing there?'

We chatted for another half an hour or so before some tea and snacks were sent up to us. We kept talking late into the evening. Then Vrindavan went downstairs to see how far the dinner preparations had proceeded.

It was quite hot inside the room, so once again I went out to take a stroll in the open air. When I arrived at the spot on the roof beneath which the bamboo structure had been created, I again felt the strong desire to jump. No one else was on the roof, so there was no one to stop me. This was the opportune moment! But at the same time I felt as if in the very depths of my mind, someone was telling me, 'Don't jump, you fool! Don't do it. You will fall to your death!' I felt a strange throbbing sensation in my head.

I can't say how much time elapsed or even what thought or incident led to another, when suddenly a cry from Vrindavan roused me from my trance. I felt him grab me by the arm and pull me away from the edge of the roof.

'What the hell is wrong with you? You almost jumped from the roof! Luckily your foot got caught in a bamboo pole. What a catastrophe it would have been!'

My head was in a whirl and my body felt restless. I said to Vrindavan, 'I don't really know what happened, brother.'

Vrindavan took me inside the room and made me lie down. Everybody said that it was probably the train journey in the heat of the day that had made me feel unwell and dizzy, and that I had fallen into a swoon and almost toppled over the edge of the roof. But I knew that I hadn't fainted. I had wilfully thrown myself from the roof, but although I tried my best to recall the moment when I decided to jump, I was unable to do so.

After I lay down on the bed for a while, I started feeling much better. Turning on one side, I suddenly felt a sharp object touch my chest. I took out the object from my pocket and saw that it was the medal that I'd borrowed from Sudhir.

Strange! All this while, I'd completely forgotten about the medal. I now showed it to Vrindavan. The other members of the household became curious and took a close look at the medal and felt it from all sides.

I returned to my house for the night. There was no one else in my house at that time. I stayed alone in one of the rooms. However, that night I noticed something. Ever since I left Vrindavan's house and started walking home, I had been feeling a strange sense of fear, which only seemed to increase when I entered my house! So many times I have spent the night alone in this house, and never have I felt any kind of fear. No, I must have been really out of sorts and unwell. When one is ill, it is only natural that the mind too becomes weak.

I switched off the lights and went to sleep. There is a large window near the head of my bedstead through which I could see the plantations at the back of the house. The moon was shining brightly—it was *Ekadashi*, the eleventh day of *Krishna Paksha*. I had kept the window open so I could get some air. I can't say how long I'd slept. It could not have been more than an hour or so—when

I suddenly awoke. I felt as if there was someone standing right outside the window, and I only had to glance in that direction to see him! At this thought, I suddenly felt a shiver run down my spine. I had no idea what it was that I feared. And yet, so strong was the fear that I simply could not bring myself to look that way. Even though I did not look, I could distinctly feel that someone had put his two hands on the window grid and was standing outside the window that very moment—fixedly looking down at me with glaring eyes. I only needed to look in that direction to see him.

My heart was in my throat, and I could feel a tremendous struggle within me. I closed my eyes and kept lying on the bed—nothing could induce me to look towards the window. I tried to put myself to sleep—but a strange and unpleasant smell seemed to emanate from close by. What was it? Had a rat died inside the house? It smelled like iodine or used lint, maybe some ointment, or something of that sort, and intermingled with that acrid smell was the smell of rotting flesh. The house stayed uninhabited for long periods of time; I realised that the caretaker wasn't doing his job of keeping the rooms clean.

A voice inside me seemed to be saying, 'Look towards the window. Why don't you *look*?'

I could feel a strange influence in the room, something that was ominous, hostile, virulent, and entirely restless, a kind of power that is difficult to convey in words. As if right then I was in deep peril! In the kind of danger that could take me to death's door—or even further, take me across to the dark hell beyond and drown me in the ice-cold stillness that lies there!

But I could not, and I would not look towards that window.

Then something within me told me that whatever malevolent influence or power it may be, within my room, on this side of the walls, it had no place. Ever since the house was built, my forefathers have regularly worshipped *Vastu shaligrams* in this room, so no one could possibly harm those residing within these four walls. Oh yes, on dark, lonely nights there is so much that your inner voice reveals to you!

A sound emanated from close to the window. A strange sound. As if someone had put money on the window sill and was trying to draw my attention! Once...twice...thrice! I felt as if my chest would burst with the fear within me. Should I cry for help? Or should I take a quick look at the window? Suddenly I remembered that many days ago, a mongoose had dug a burrow underneath the outer wall below the window latch. I'd caught sight of it once that evening as well. It must have been busy at that nocturnal hour, hunting for insects and fireflies on the window frame, and that is what must be causing this sound that I heard.

As soon as I remembered this, my courage seemed to revive. Oh, the peril was finally over! When one is unwell, what strange fancies enter the mind! And the most ordinary occurrences give rise to a disproportionate amount of fear! Turning to one side, I heaved a sigh of relief and tried to go back to sleep. But this relieved state of mind did not last long. I simply could not convince myself that I was alone there that night. There was someone else close by—I could feel it. With sleepless eyes, he was keeping a close watch on me, determined to deprive me of a restful night.

Time and again I would doze off, only to have my slumber interrupted and I would come awake once again, but try as I might I could not find the courage to glance towards the open window or to sit up on my bed. At short intervals I could hear the scraping sound from the window, which I now thought was the very soft sound of the latch. That sound seemed to say to me, 'Look towards the window...Turn and look towards the window...'

I noticed I had been sweating profusely...such sultry weather this time of the year! I spent the long night in this condition before dawn finally broke through. The early morning light gradually permeated the room, bringing with it the sounds of fellow human beings, and with that the fear of the night finally dissipated. With a mind free of troubles, I was eventually able to get some rest and I slept till nine. I woke up, had my tea and then left the house to take a stroll down the para.

Something happened at that point which back then I didn't think was significant. But later on, when I reflected on the sequence of events, it did seem quite astonishing. My jaetha-moshai (whom I've mentioned previously) stays close by in the same locality. While I was on my stroll, I saw him coming from the other side of the street. When I'd left the house last evening, I'd taken the medal along to show him, but due to the invitation from Vrindavan and as a consequence of having to stay back till late in the night to have dinner with him, I hadn't been able to meet my jaetha-moshai.

On catching sight of me, he said, 'Hey! Suren...how are you doing? I realised you'd come. Saw you yesterday, late in the evening. It was quite late, so I didn't call out. You were returning from Vrindavan's place, I believe. I was taking my after-dinner stroll on the roof. It was quite hot and stuffy yesterday. I noticed that you were with another person, so I did not feel it was right to call out to you. Who was that person? Such a tall fellow...like a Sikh or a Punjabi...a friend of yours, is he? One doesn't usually get to see such a physique amongst Bengalis.'

I stared at my jaetha-moshai in astonishment, and said, 'A tall person accompanying me on the way back to the house last night! What is that you say?'

Hearing my words, he seemed even more astonished than I was, and said, 'You were not accompanied by anyone you say? You were all alone? Son, has my eyesight deteriorated to such an extent all of a sudden?!'

I laughed and said, 'That must be it, Jaetha-moshai. Your eyes must have deceived you. You have grown older now! There was no one accompanying me. Moreover, the mango tree in front of your house throws a shadow, and the intermingling of darkness and light must have played tricks with your vision. Such things do happen.'

Jaetha-moshai appeared considerably bewildered on hearing my words. He said, 'How very strange! Can my eyes be so mistaken?'

'When you came to the other side of the mango tree,' he continued, 'you turned on your torch. At that moment I clearly saw you and a tall man standing behind you. Thereafter, you switched off the torch and entered the area that was dark with the shadow of the mango tree. Even then I could distinctly make out in the moonlight that the man followed you towards the house. He stood almost a hand taller than you...he was there, right behind you. But of course, from this distance and in that darkness so late in the evening I wasn't able to see the details of his appearance too clearly. I even thought of calling out and asking you who your friend was. Can it be that my sight can misguide me so much?' he finished, looking quite perplexed.

I had to explain to him again that there was no one accompanying me yesterday. I was all alone; hence what he saw must surely be ascribed to his weakening eyesight. There was no other conclusion to be drawn from this.

I spent the rest of the day with Vrindavan. The happenings of the night and the fact that I'd spent it shuddering with fear now seemed to me as such a laughable and embarrassing matter that I did not venture to speak to Vrindavan about it.

I decided to take the late evening train back to Calcutta. By the time I returned to my village home after having evening tea with Vrindavan, and picked up my suitcase, dusk had already fallen. I made my way through the large plantation of Bauri Para—it takes almost five or six minutes to cross it. Halfway through the plantation, God knows what occurred to me, I turned around and looked back. As soon as I did, a flash of lightning seemed to pass through me and a sudden fear turned my entire body to stone.

Who was that standing there?

In the half light of dusk, I could make out a strange form standing on one side of the road, in the midst of dense shrubs—a towering figure, with a tall *topee* made of horse hair on his head. The topee was held together with a thin chain of steel going around the chin, the kind one usually sees in photographs on the heads of *gora* soldiers! The figure seemed to be standing absolutely motionless, staring at me! Hardly ten yards away from me, or it could have been less! Heart in my mouth, I took a few steps towards him, as if I simply had to gratify this eerie inquisitiveness! The figure stood completely still, like a statue of stone. I saw the figure standing there looking at me, barely seven or eight yards away now. The topee of horse hair and the steel chain were clearly visible.

My legs started shivering, my body started growing numb, and I suddenly began to feel very light-headed! I think if I'd kept standing there for another half-minute or so, I might even have fallen into a swoon because at that moment, I found myself standing face-to-face with that terrible figure—I could feel my legs turning impossibly heavy and weighing me down. There seemed no way to uproot myself from that spot...

But just then, a few people seemed to enter the plantation with lanterns in their hands. On hearing some human sounds, my courage seemed to revive and I cried out for help. They rushed to my side. Seeing me standing there alone in the midst of the jungle they were much surprised, and asked me, 'What is the matter, *Babu*? What did you see?'

They shone their lanterns in my face and recognising me, they said 'Oh, it's you! What's the matter? Your face is all white and pale. Did you get a fright or what? This Bauri Bagan is not a good place to be so late in the evening. After dusk, many people tend to feel unsafe here.'

In the light of the lanterns, I saw that the figure was still standing there—in the same position as before! One of the men said, 'What did you see? Was it that pineapple tree?'

Another person said, 'They have pruned the branches of that tree. Now with that bush-shaped structure sitting on top, one may easily mistake it for a human figure. Come away from this spot, Babu.'

I too was able to make out now that it was but a pineapple tree. With its leaves pruned, the top of the tree looked just like a topee worn by the Horse Guards! One's sight can play such bizarre tricks! And to think that it was me, just the day before too, who was suggesting to jaetha-moshai that he get a new pair of glasses! I felt embarrassed at the thought. He was an elderly person and it was perfectly understandable that his eyes could mislead him—especially considering how I myself had been so deceived!

With their lanterns lighting the way, the people guided me to the station.

The next day at school, I returned Sudhir's medal to him.

Sudhir said, 'Dadu has asked you to come to our place. Will you accompany me after school gets over today?'

When I met Sudhir's grandfather later that day, he said, 'Thank heavens! I was really worried about you, Master Babu! I got to know that you'd taken the medal with you to your village. I didn't know your address in the village, or else I would have sent a telegram. That medal was given to my father by a gora soldier. I wasn't even born then. The man had given it to my father as collateral but had never been able to claim it back. He was a rash fellow and a drunkard. That medal is an object of danger. If a person from a *family* other than ours takes that medal, he may experience great peril. Many years back, much against my advice, a brother-in-law of mine once took the medal away with him to show it to his family; that very same day he fell to his death from the roof of his house. The medal was found in his pocket.'

Like a mechanised puppet, I was only able to utter, 'From the roof? The medal was found in his pocket?'

'That's right, Master Babu. My own brother-in-law. Why would I lie? It's been almost twenty-seven or twenty-eight years now. A few other people had also taken it away with them, but they had hastened to return it to me. They said they felt terrified in the evenings and at night, and that their body and mind started to grow numb. They felt as if someone was following them. Possession of this medal cannot be endured by a person who does not belong to our family. Their life will be in imminent danger. That's why I was thinking of dispatching a telegram to you.'

There is something I must say here. About a month after my return to Calcutta, I happened to visit my village again. On entering Bauri Bagan, I went to the spot where I'd been so terrified that night and looked in the direction where I'd seen the figure. I could see no trace of a pineapple tree anywhere near. Instead, there was a mango tree beside which that pineapple tree should have been. Time and again I returned to that spot to look for it, but I couldn't find that tree. Assuming that it had been cut down in the interim, there would at least have been the bole or some remnant of the tree, but there were no such signs. Looking at that spot, it didn't seem as if a large pineapple tree could ever have stood there...

Previously published in Bengali as *'Medal'* in *Bibhutibhushan Golpo Shomogro*.

The Mountains of Kushal

That year at the end of the month of *Bhadra* I had gone on a vacation to Manoharpur, which is adjacent to the forested state of Sundergarh. Manoharpur is surrounded on all sides by hill ranges. I had come for a two-day visit and intended to stay at the *dak bungalow* there. But I happened to meet a Bengali gentleman who'd been staying in Manoharpur for quite some time now. He simply wouldn't let go of me and insisted on taking me home.

I said to him, 'You'll be inconvenienced. I might stay on here for a long time.'

He laughed softly and gave a long sigh of comfort. 'Thank God! Will you stay for more than two months?'

'No,' I said.

'Do stay! Why don't you?'

'No,' I said again.

'Why do you hesitate so much? In Bengal, a Bengali may or may not be another Bengali's friend, but when you are elsewhere that's how it must be. Do stay as long as you wish to, and please think of it as your own house.'

One day, my host Manmatha *Babu* said, 'Satish Babu, would you like to go to a nice place?'

'Where is this place?' I asked.

'It is in a thickly forested area and not easily accessible. We'll have to go by bullock cart. I know of a good sadhu who lives there,' he answered.

The place he was referring to was Bhairav Sthan or God's Abode, around seventeen miles from Manoharpur, deep within the mountains of Kushal.

'I'm not quite in need of any sadhus or *sanyasis*,' I said, 'but what is the jungle there like?'

'It is incredible.'

'Then I'll surely go.'

Sundergarh is a heavenly forest, lush and green. At every step one encounters the forest floor turned into a bed of petals from the fallen flowers of the *kadam* tree. Long-beaked hornbills and wild parakeets can be seen hovering around the branches. In one place you can see the golden yellow rays of the early morning sun clothing the mountain peaks; at another, you may find that *lohajaali* flowers blooming on the edge of the waters of a mountain spring have completely hidden the backdrop of rocks. The path seems endless and the forest appears limitless, and every way you look you see verdant fields nestling in the lap of tall mountains. The jungle is full of peacocks, barking deer, bears and leopards.

The bullock cart was making its way through the forest path at a sluggish pace. Sometimes we were lumbering up a steep hillside flanked by the fruit-laden branches of *aamloki* trees. At another time we caught sight of a glen, strewn with jujubes fallen from the overhanging trees, gently undulating towards a forest stream overflowing with fresh water. The crest of the Kali Pahadi or Black Hill could be seen emerging from the midst of the dense underlying jungle like the conical peak of Mount Vesuvius.

We'd left by bullock cart early in the morning. We carried with us parched rice, sugar, bananas, curd, ripe papayas, home-made *kheer-sondesh* and pickles. On the way, we gathered ripe gooseberries of an enormous size, forest figs and *shaak*. The beauty of the forest during the monsoons can hardly be described. I didn't want the journey to come to an end because that would mean the magic would end too. Once again I would be thrown in the midst of human habitation, black marketing, newspapers, desist-from-eating-rice-at-least-once-a-week kind of advice, the refugee problem, and so on. In the midst of this beautiful magical forest, I wanted the bullock cart to go on as long as it could.

It was twelve noon.

A woodland river, brought to life by the plentiful rains, had formed a miniature waterfall that gurgled and cascaded exuberantly through the forest shadows.

I asked my companion, 'Which river is that, *Moshai*?'

'A branch of the Koel river,' Manmatha Babu answered.

'South Koel, you mean?'

'Yes, of course. I will show you a kind of stone that is found in the waters of this river. It has a beautiful colour, like Chinese jade. Come, there is a large rock nearby. We can sit there and have some food.'

'How many times have you been to this place?' I asked.

'Four times,' he replied, 'to meet the sadhu of Bhairav Sthan. You'll see he is no ordinary sadhu. He will inspire your respect and veneration.

I should have said 'Yours as well.' (You've already heard my opinion of sadhus.)

We reached the massive rock and spread a *chuddar* on it for us to sit. Our hunger had been stirred. We had started feeling so ravenous that our stomachs seemed to be burning and crying out for food. The fare we had brought along seemed insubstantial. It appeared that the water in these parts had magical and curative properties. I had been suffering from indigestion all this past year and here I was, looking forward to eating. We ate parched rice mixed with curd, and together with the various fruits that we had at our disposal, it was a pretty nice meal. We drank the clear water from the waterfall and boarded the cart to continue onwards. During this leg of our journey, we started walking since it can be quite cumbersome to travel in a bullock cart for a long period in jungle terrain.

In these forest glades overhung with gentle shadows, the cool air carried the sweet fragrance of wildflowers in all directions, turning the heart and mind somnolent. The deep, secluded and timeless forest-path felt like a cool arbour at every step of the way.

Everywhere you looked there was a delightful profusion of birds, and you could hear the call of doves from the top branches of the trees. In the blue sky above, white clouds floated away. Thankfully, there was no rain.

A thought came to mind. Far away from city life, these forest paths are safe and entirely free of danger. The tribes that inhabit these forests have no understanding of theft or burglary. My companion said, 'You can leave your money with these people, and whether you know them or not you can always come back and find it safe. I know this and can vouch for it.'

'Don't they accost you on the paths and harm you? Don't they have revolvers or crude bombs?'

'They've never even heard of such things.'

'How do they make a living? There are no signs of cultivation.'

'The *Birhor* tribe forms the bulk of the people inhabiting these parts. That bean is what they primarily eat,' Manmatha Babu said, pointing to a creeper on a tree. 'They plant the beans and let the creepers grow on the trees. They also eat birds, hares, lizards, snakes, and other such creatures. They're satisfied with very little and have no desire for hard labour. They will sometimes consume a lot of *mahua tari* and then sleep for three days! Also, they hardly understand the value of currency.'

Close to the forest path, almost concealed by the forest, we came across the hut of a Birhor family. The men of the house were not in, and the women were pounding rice. Bestowed with beautiful, strong physiques, their entire person glistened with the appearance of good health, their smiles unabashed and radiant on their faces. There was no other hut close by. The ones that we could see were a fair distance away from each other. A city-bred Bengali woman would never be able to stay with her children in such a hut amidst these dense forests even for a day. The minds of city folk, made weak by long exposure to civilisation, will on the very first day be numbed by the fear of tigers and bears and ghosts.

Those of us who live in the city can hardly comprehend how civilisation has made us dull and weary. One cannot grasp the strength, vigour and endurance of hardship that is required of the free life in the forest when standing in the queue to board a tram. Only today was I able to appreciate this.

The creepers were swinging gently in the thickets. The skyline lit up with hues of warm red and orange, and the tree-tops became suffused with the light. It was around this time that we reached Bhairav Sthan.

My companion asked, 'Are we carrying mosquito nets with us?'

'No,' I responded.

'Then what do we do?'

'Are there a lot of mosquitoes here?'

'It seems so.'

'I have some incense sticks in my suitcase. We can light those,' I said. Then I asked, 'Where will we stay?'

'There is a room that is empty,' he said. 'I will ask the cart driver to take some straw and clean it up. And at night, we can cook our dinner.'

'Fine by me. This will be a picnic of sorts. Wish I had brought the girls along. There would've been much gaiety with them here,' I said thinking of my wife and my young daughters, who would certainly have enjoyed this trip.

'During *Poornima*, a fair will be held here. You can bring *Ma Lakshmi* from Calcutta then. That will be an excellent time,' he advised.

'Won't we get to meet Sadhuji now?' I asked.

'Yes, certainly we will. Come, let's put our abode in order first. Then we'll go,' he said.

The lodging was finalised. We didn't need to do much cleaning; seeing some holes in the floor, however, we were worried. In the monsoons, such holes may turn out to be the home of venomous snakes. My companion said, 'Don't be so afraid. Let's first get done with our cooking.'

We spoke to a *Santhal* man named Mangal Tudu about the possibility of procuring some firewood for our cooking. He agreed to bring us some for the paltry sum of four paise. He asked us where we were staying.

'At the playhouse,' we replied.

'But why?' he asked. You could have gone to the *Ghatoyali* bungalow. The sahib's bungalow is kept open for folks like you. Come, I will take you there,' he said.

After bringing us some wood and water, Mangal Tudu helped us to prepare our meals. After we had eaten, we went to the Ghatoyali bungalow. By that time, it was already an hour or two past dusk.

Although the bungalow was built of straw, the floor was made of cement. Chairs, tables and cots were all arranged properly in the room, and there were curtains as well over the doors and windows. The Ghatoyali *zamindar* government of the place had set it up for the stay of high-ranking forest department officials and had been continuing to maintain the place, not by choice but out of compulsion from Ghatoyali laws, rules and regulations. Although we were not government officials, the fact that we are Bengali gentlemen somehow entitled us to use the bungalow. The *chowkidar* greeted us with a *salaam* and opened the rooms for us.

Next, we went to meet the sadhu. Mangal Tudu accompanied us to the sadhu's place. He informed us that the sadhu was a great man—and that he kept silent during the day and ventured to speak only after dusk.

I was quite amazed when I saw the sadhu. Around seventy, with a flowing white beard, a *tulsi-mala* around his neck, and a strong and healthy physique, the sadhu had large, peaceful eyes bestowing fatherly love. He was originally from Bengal, hailing from the district of Manbhum. At the age of seventeen, he left home and had since then become indifferent to the charms that society had to offer. He spoke frankly, disclosing the details of his past to us. The obscurity and ambiguity (stemming from an inherent sense of pride) that is so often apparent in sadhus were missing in him. He sat on a wide, smooth rock with his back resting against the trunk of a massive and ancient *sal* tree. The moonlight of *Shukla Navami* filtering through the branches and foliage of the trees fell on the *asana* on which he sat. Looking around, as far as the eyes could see the mountain ranges of Kushal surrounded Bhairav Sthan on all sides. The rocks were all very old, dating back many aeons. In fact, everything there seemed ancient—a venerable sadhu, a timeless sal tree, an ancient rock serving as the sadhu's asana, and all around, the antediluvian forest! My heart tells me to never leave this place, to stay back here. The divine light of *rishis* and sadhus may be availed here. I'll never find it anywhere else. Here in this distant forest in Sundergarh resides this venerable, fatherly, loving and *brahmagya* rishi to whose proximity I've been brought today; he'll bring everlasting peace to my mind. One doesn't come across such a rare blessing easily.

I was all the more fascinated when the sadhu uttered a *shloka* from the *Upanishads* and then proceeded to interpret it for our benefit. '*Kavirmanishi paribhu swayambhu*', he said, again and again. His solemn words still sound in my ears today:

'He is indeed a poet. I sit here and observe. The sal tree bears flowers; during the monsoons, peacocks can be heard calling in the mountains; water flows gently down in the jungle streams, and this makes me think that He is indeed a poet. There is nothing I've gained, really. Whatever you see on my outer body is false. I've hardly gained any knowledge. But yes, I've had this desire to see Him. And getting to see Him like this—embodied as a poet—I feel gratified and blessed.'

What I've related occurred around seven years back.

Returning to Calcutta, I once again slipped into the morning-to-evening office routine. The money I have is not sufficient to allow me to take myself away on a vacation every year or as and when I wish to.

I went to a party the other day. It was a party hosted by someone quite rich. I saw many people arrive in Chryslers, Buicks and Minervas. They were all well turned-out and had attractive faces and personalities.

But in this gathering of educated, aristocratic people, did I find what I'd expected to find? Not at all. I only got to hear materialistic conversations that went like this:

'I couldn't go to the house at Deoghar this time around. My elder son wanted to stock it up with some more furniture, so I bought some and had it sent over there. Last time round no one from the family went there. Neither did they go this year. I may not keep it anymore because I can't find the time to go there at all, and nor do the boys. The broker Bishanlal had quoted a price of forty thousand rupees in March. My wife doesn't wish to sell the house. And yet, we're hardly ever able to go and stay there.'

'What about you? Did you construct something in your land at Regent Park?'

'Yes, I have sent the plan for approval. Mr Bagchi has given us an estimate of more than eighty thousand. They're the ones who will do it. Mr P. Ghoshal's house was constructed by Bagchi. He has done an amazing job.'

Or else there were conversations like this one.

'What do you make of all this unrest amongst the labour class just before the elections?'

'Not good. It's the same everywhere. The parties that won't take their side will be in trouble during the elections.'

'Yes, that is quite evident. The emergence of such conflict in the country and the forming of these groups and factions will only...'

And so the conversation went on, followed by a lengthy political analysis.

Sitting there in that electrified ambience, amongst well-dressed and well-educated gentlemen, my thoughts went back to the words of that ancient sage in the mountains of Kushal—his beautiful, simple utterances made in that secluded place surrounded by forests. My mind took me back to that place and time. That beautiful day's half-remembered memories sounded in my ears like the verses of a sweet and delightful song.

There was something else that the sadhu had said. Uttered in that beautiful forest ambience, surrounded by tall sals turned green at the end of Bhadra, how sublime and wondrous his words had seemed. Such profound and significant words.

He had said: 'The conception of liberty is based on the assumption that we are confined. If we reason carefully, we will see that man neither has liberty nor is he confined. *Brahma* is an unknown kingdom. The one who goes there realises that Brahma is neither godly nor ungodly. Brahma is beyond the *Shastra*s, beyond contention and dispute, attainable neither through godliness nor through ungodliness! It's all about perception. Man is free. It's just that he is not aware of it. Yes, man is forever free. One doesn't need to read anything, nor does one need to cultivate a particular practice. One's own perception and experience is an adventurer and in itself serves as the explorer that can, in an instant, propel one to the enlightened world of liberty and salvation! Believe me when I say that Man is free. He himself has tied himself up. He himself needs to experience that he is free! He is Man, He is Free.'

Previously published in Bengali as '*Kushal Pahadi*' in *Bibhutibhushan Golpo Shomogro*.

The Bodiless

We were having quite a curious conversation that day when we had all gathered under the litchi tree. Talk was mostly centred around some insipid ghost stories about village ghosts clad in white that people tend to come across sometimes in the bamboo forests and mango orchards in rural areas. Such stories have been told and heard many a time. No one had anything other than these to offer.

Just then, Sarat Chakraborty joined our gathering. After working for long years in the excise department, he has since retired. He must be around sixty. He explores Tantric practices these days and also prepares horoscopes for people free of charge. In addition, he provides advice regarding precious stones, more specifically, about which stone may be auspicious for a particular person. It is rare to find someone working in the field of astrology for the benefit of others, with no thought of gain to oneself. He is a perfect gentleman, and people revere him. Out of respect, many do not even venture to smoke in his presence.

Sarat *Babu* came into our midst and said, 'Hello, what's up today? Such a cloudy day. Looks like rain is imminent!'

Shyamapada Moktar said, 'Come, please come, Chakraborty *Moshai*. We're exchanging ghost stories on this cloudy day. But they are not all that interesting. You must have...'

Sarat Chakraborty said, 'I can tell you a story, but it is not a ghost story. What category of story it is I cannot exactly say. You may listen to it and then decide for yourselves.'

On that overcast day heaven and earth seemed to have fused together as one, so dense were the clouds. We settled down to listen to Sarat Babu's story.

Sarat Babu said, 'I was once suddenly transferred to the Dooars Belt, beyond Jalpaiguri. Back then, my family was putting up in Dhaka. Leaving them there, I left for Jalpaiguri. This was an entirely new region for me, so without first taking stock of the place, it wasn't sensible to take my family along. Also, my children were in school in Dhaka at the time.

'The place I was posted to was quite a distance away from Jalpaiguri. To reach there, I had to travel by narrow-gauge train. Looking out of the train windows, I could see tea gardens on either side. It is a heavily forested belt, but far away, beyond the forest line, one can see the Himalayas. It's a very secluded and remote area. The place I had to report to was called Holdia. When I reached there, I was put up at the residence of the senior sub-inspector, the reason being that my own residence hadn't been finalised yet. This gentleman's name was Rebatimohan Mukherjee. He hailed from the district of Nadia. He was fair-complexioned, tall and well-built. He took good care of me and assured me that within a few days a house would be found for me.

'On the morning of the third day, Rebati Babu said, "There is something I should tell you."

'"What is it?" I asked.

'"You've made a mistake coming here at this time."

'"Why do you say so?"

'"Haven't you heard about the occurrences in these parts?"

'"No," I said. "What are you talking about?"

'"During this rainy season, people are falling ill from the terrible blackwater fever. You are new to these parts, so the probability of you catching it is even more. Once you catch the fever a few times, susceptibility to blackwater increases. And when that happens, one's life is in danger. This is the dreadful state of affairs in this part of the country."

'"Then how are you people able to manage here?"

'"There's not much use going into that. I'm not staying here willingly. One has to do something to feed oneself. That's why I'm here. If I leave my job, where will I go, and what will I eat? Two of my daughters have died of blackwater fever. Even then, I haven't been able to secure a transfer to another place. You tell me, what can I do, Sarat Babu?"

'"Yes, I understand," I said.

'"If you take some precautions, it will suffice. You should never drink water that has not been boiled, even when you are away from home."

'"Do those who contract the blackwater fever always die?"

'"If you don't receive good treatment, the chances of survival are very slim. Especially if someone new to these parts contracts the fever during the monsoon, it is very difficult to save the person. I've seen two such cases—both of them died."

'I felt some amount of dread on hearing this. Would precautions alone be sufficient, I wondered? In a faraway land, how much care is adequate and how much care can one possibly take? Submitting myself to fate and destiny, I started my work. I began going to various places within a distance of ten to twelve miles, inspecting liquor shops and shops selling cannabis.

'I was having a pleasant stay. The jungles had started turning green with the advent of the rains. Flowers of innumerable varieties were in bloom. There were so many different species of birds whose calls could be heard. Once, on the distant horizon, I was able to see a snow-capped peak of the Himalayas shining in the early morning sun like a mound of candy. Later, due to the bright sunlight it could no longer be seen.

'Meanwhile, through Rebati Babu's efforts, a comfortable dwelling was found for me. Wooden planks had been laid on top of wooden stilts and a kind of bungalow had been built on it. The wooden flooring was quite dry and free of dampness, and the rooms were spacious, with plenty of light and good ventilation.

'The fear in my heart gradually receded. I remember thinking that it hadn't been judicious of Rebati Babu to have made me so afraid, and that too when I'd barely arrived in Holdia. Why did

Rebati Babu do so? Did he have any ulterior motive in saying what he did? I started thinking on such lines.

'I happened to find myself a Brahmin orderly. His name was Digambar Pandey, and he'd lived in those parts for a long time. He was a good cook and took care of the shopping as well. I didn't face any discomfort.

'After a month or two I went on an excise inspection to a place known as Bamnapara North. It was a small bazaar close to a tea garden. At the entrance to the tea garden was a hoarding that said "Bamnapara North Tea Estate". After crossing a small mountain river, my bullock cart entered the bazaar. It was around ten in the morning. Two *Marwari* tradesmen trading in forest produce had their shops there. A merchant from Medinipur, named Deben Samant, had set up his timber business there. The shops selling cannabis and opium were owned by Deben Samant's brother, Shashi Samant.

'While I was there at the bazaar, I started feeling somewhat unwell and developed a headache as well. When I mentioned this to Deben Samant, he gave me a homoeopathic medicine saying, "This will cure you. There is nothing for you to fear."

'I asked him, "Have you had cases of blackwater fever here?"

'"A lot," he said.

'"And do people die of it?"

'"Yes, quite a few of them."

'"Are you not afraid of catching the disease?" I asked.

'"We've been here a long time. Those who are new to these parts, they are more at risk," he replied.

'Everybody seemed to say the same thing. By the time I got down to checking the accounts of cannabis sales, I felt so indisposed that I couldn't sit anymore. I somehow managed to finish my task, and got on to the bullock cart. Feeling thirsty, I asked the tea garden's Nepali gatekeeper, who lived in a shed, for some water.

'By the time I reached my house, it was past noon, and I had developed a high fever. I had been shivering all the way back from Bamnapara. On hearing about my ill health, Rebati Babu came over to see me. He called for a doctor. Medicines and injections followed. Within three days the fever dissipated.

'The next two weeks went well.

'Everybody said that I might have caught a cold which had probably brought on the illness. That was all there was to it.

'I too convinced myself along similar lines. Once again I started working. I did not feel any signs of weariness. One day, I was sitting at the Holdia police station and chatting with the assistant sub-inspector when I suddenly started feeling feverish. The sub-inspector arranged for someone to accompany me back to my place.

'When I reached home, I asked Digambar Pandey to give me some water. After drinking it, I went and lay down. For three days I suffered with terribly high fever. Rebati Babu and the assistant sub-inspector would both come to see me in the mornings and evenings. They gave exact instructions to my orderly on how *shaboo* and barley had to be prepared. After three days, the fever reduced.

'Gradually, I recovered and went back to work. Around fifteen days later, I'd gone to investigate an excise-related case at the tea garden when suddenly I fell ill again. This time around, there was something I noticed. The fever that occurs in this remote forested area appears in the body suddenly, and then disappears equally abruptly. Therefore, the fear that I had initially felt when I fell ill didn't take hold of me this time. Calling my orderly, I instructed him to make the food and the concoctions that he'd already learnt to prepare.

'But events unfolded somewhat differently this time.

'I wasn't able to get rid of the illness easily. Within two days I started displaying all the symptoms of the virulent blackwater fever. Due to excessive blood loss, I became extremely weak. It took me five or six days to recover, after which I had to follow a convalescent's diet. I was on this diet for two days, when on the morning of the third day, Rebati Babu and the assistant sub-inspector came to meet me. I asked my orderly to prepare some tea, but they declined to have any. Later on, I remember thinking that they refused the tea probably because they considered blackwater fever to be an infectious disease. The assistant sub-inspector said, "Sarat Babu, may I say something?"

'"Yes, please," I said.

'"You should leave this place."

'"Why do you say so?"

'"That is what the doctor says you must do."

'"But he hasn't said anything to me," I objected.

'The assistant sub-inspector hesitantly said, "No, he hasn't mentioned it to you. He has asked us to convey his advice to you instead. He said that your affliction is quite serious. Meaning that..."

'"But I've already recovered," I interrupted him.

'"Recovering from this condition is very tough, Sarat Babu," the man said.

'"Fine," I replied, "but how will I reach the station? I don't see any way of getting past Rammyaghat."

'"You need not worry," said the assistant sub-inspector. "We're arranging for a stretcher from the tea garden. We'll send a porter along. A police constable will also accompany you. They will not return until they see you have safely boarded the train."

'"Okay, that's fine with me," I said, giving in.

'I didn't realise then that that could have been the last day of my life, but I'll come to that a little later.

'Once I had given my consent, the sub-inspector left.

'It must have been nine in the morning. I asked my orderly to bring some hot water for me so that I could wash my hands and feet. Thereafter, I ate some barley. Later in the day, I had some rice as well. Post noon, some people arrived carrying a stretcher.'

At this point, Sarat Babu said, 'I feel like having some tea.'

We said, 'Please complete the story first,' loath to have the narrative interrupted.

'I'll continue after having some tea. I've reached the crux of the story now, so let me moisten my throat before I continue,' Sarat Babu said firmly.

The lawyer Nitaipada Raha interjected, 'You said that you'd fallen ill with blackwater fever, and then recovered; in spite of that the doctor had opined that you were not well. How is that?'

'You will understand this when I continue with my story. Actually, I had not recovered.'

'Then why did the doctor recommend a diet meant for convalescents?'

'I can't quite say. I didn't ask anyone then myself. But what I am narrating to you is exactly what took place,' Sarat Babu said.

'This is an astonishing thing you're saying, Moshai. I can't understand what kind of doctors operate in those parts!' said Nitai Babu.

'Well, I've never actually thought about this until you mentioned it. Anyway, now let me tell you the rest of it.' Sarat Chakraborty then continued with his story.

'As I was saying, sometime after twelve, a few people arrived from the tea garden, carrying a stretcher. Both Rebati Babu and the assistant sub-inspector were present. My orderly and I were packing and putting things in order when I started feeling feverish again. A horrible shivering kind of fever. I was unable to sit. Going back to my room, I asked the orderly to unpack my sleeping sack and lay down. I hardly knew what took place next. My entire consciousness seemed to have been extinguished by a dense darkness.

'When I regained my senses, there were two things I noticed. First, I could see the branch of a tree swinging in the breeze in the darkness outside my window. Secondly, my trunk and bundle had been kept near my feet, adjacent to the wall, and my chest was resting against a wall-like structure.

'Have I boarded a train? But why is the compartment so dark? Why aren't there other people in the compartment?

'Thereafter, gradually the clouds started clearing from my mind. I recalled that I hadn't got on the stretcher at all, but feeling feverish and unwell, I had entered my room and lain down.

'But if it was my room, then where was my orderly, Digambar? And why have the lights been put off? Where exactly am I?

'I was feeling thirsty. I got up to call for my orderly. But the words were stuck in my throat. Twice I tried, and it was the same each time.

'It looked like the moon had risen. A little moonlight had entered the room through the window. For a little while, I kept looking straight in front of me. I could hear no sound either within the house or outside it.

'Suddenly my glance was drawn outside the window. Who was there?

'Recalling the scene even after so many years, I still get goose bumps. Do you know what I saw? A dark girl was walking rapidly around the house, and using a stick that she held in her hand she was doing something with it on the ground. Through the crack in my door, I saw her going around the house twice. After the third time, drawing herself up, the girl suddenly looked at me and said, "There is nothing to fear. I am drawing a line and cordoning off the area. Tonight, no one will be able to enter inside. You go to sleep now."

'I saw the girl for a very short time. Thereafter, I sensed that she had gone to the other side of the house. I may have lost consciousness then or perhaps I had fallen asleep.

'How long I slept before I woke again, I cannot exactly say. But when I did, I saw the dark girl sitting close to my bedstead. She didn't seem to be more than eighteen. There was something else I noticed. The girl seemed to be sweating profusely. Her face was marked by drops of sweat. Her entire body seemed to be covered with perspiration.

'The moment I glanced at her, she spoke in the most serene and loving voice, "Why did you wake up? Sleep, sleep...There is nothing to fear...go to sleep..."

'At the sound of her words, I once again fell into a slumber. Before falling asleep, my eyes were drawn to the branch of the tree outside the window. With the moonlight falling on it, it was clearly visible now.

'My story kind of ends here.

'When I woke up early next morning, I felt as if I was doing so in a natural state of health and well-being. I felt no illness or fatigue, but I could tell that my body had grown weak. I wasn't able to get up from my bed.

'Gradually, the day began to dawn. I saw Digambar Pandey hesitantly making his way towards the house and peeping inside.

When I called out to him, for a moment he seemed to be shocked out of his wits. I told him to go and call Rebati Babu. With a puzzled look on his face, he went to do as I'd asked. After a while, many people arrived to see me. Rebati Babu was also amongst them.

'Rebati Babu said, "How're you, Sarat Babu?"

'"I'm fine," I said. "I would like something to eat."

'Rebati Babu immediately went out and spoke to someone. In a little while, a bowl of barley was brought in for me. After eating the barley, I felt some strength return to my body. The doctor came and examined me and said that the fever had left.

'In two days, I recovered completely from my state of ill health. I also started taking the recommended convalescent's diet. I came to know that on that terrible night, knowing that I was near death, everyone had left me alone. Doctor Babu had said that I wouldn't last the night. Who would go to my cremation in the morning, where the wood for the pyre would be procured from—all this had been discussed and arranged for! Early in the morning, a constable was to go and dispatch a telegram to my family informing them of my passing away. The assistant sub-inspector had planned for this essential task as well.

'And yet, left in that friendless, forsaken condition, who was it that had been with me, sitting near my deathbed all night long? Who was it that had cordoned off the house to save me from any and every possible danger that I could be vulnerable to in that condition? Who was it that had watched over me that night as I lay helpless and abandoned? I won't be able to answer any of these questions.

'If you say that I'd dreamt the entire episode in a feverish state of delirium, I will neither remonstrate nor will I contradict you. If indeed it was a dream, it must be said that what my consciousness had seen in that near-death state was a sweet and glorious dream, one that will remain before my eyes forever and enrich my entire life. It left in my soul a prodigious message of hope.'

Sarat Chakraborty fell silent. Tears seemed to glisten in his eyes.

Lawyer Nitai Babu asked, 'How long did you continue to stay in Holdia after this?'

'As long as the government chose to keep me there—around two years.'

'Did you continue to stay in that same house, alone all the while?'

'Only I and Digambar, no one else.'

'Did you ever see anything of that sort again?'

'No.'

'And did you suffer from any ill health?'

'No.'

It was going to be a night of heavy rainfall. It became quite dark. Fireflies could be seen in the foliage and branches of the *shiuli* tree in the yard. We were silent for quite a long time. Nitai Babu also didn't speak much. The rains were going to come down any moment, so we handed Sarat Babu an umbrella and saw him on his way.

Previously published in Bengali as '*Oshoriri*' in *Bibhutibhushan Golpo Shomogro*.

Grandma

I have come to my maternal uncle's home after a long, long time. I think it must be twenty years or more. The whole village seems to have been taken over by the jungle. Large houses are lying in a state of neglect and ruin; banyan and *peepal* trees have taken root in the fissures of roofs and walls. Doves have built their nests in the attics. Tigers can be heard calling in the night and wild boars are known to seek shelter in the jungles that have grown in the courtyards.

Many people who previously lived in the village have long since left and have found work or set up businesses in faraway places outside Bengal, where they have subsequently built their homes and live with their families. They don't wish to return to these malaria-prone villages. Their fathers and *jethus* probably visited the village in the early years, when the young migrants started their professional lives, to organise and celebrate Durga Puja and Shyama Puja. They have now grown old and turned senile, and the new generation of sons and daughters that was born in those distant lands hardly knows about their ancestral village. Some of the young people may have come here once or twice when they were children, while others may not have come at all. What attachment can possibly bring them to these villages?

As a consequence, many large houses are lying in a dilapidated state. The verandahs have broken down, even though the locks on the doors are still in place. Due to the fear of snakes, no one approaches these dwellings at any time of the day.

I saw Anadi *Mama*'s house from the outside. I remember it was in this residence that I'd first heard a gramophone in my childhood. Anadi Mama's father, Hari *Dadamoshai*, was a man of many interests, and used to work in Calcutta. He was the first person to bring this twentieth-century wonder from Calcutta to the village.

Sateesh Mama's son Jadu said, 'Hey, Kanu, come, let's go and see the *gramofono*.'

'What is that?' I asked.

'Gramofono!' Jadu repeated. 'The machine that can sing! It's in Hari *Jaetha*'s house.'

We went running to my Mama's place. On top of the wooden box was a small horn. From within the horn came the precise notes of a song sung by a human!

A small boy asked, 'Who is in there?'

'Why, what makes you think there is someone inside that horn?'

'Then who is it that sings?' the little boy countered.

'It is the machine that is emitting the sound of the song. This is called the machine's song.'

Ramtaran Chakraborty, so old that he seemed like a man from another era, had somehow made his way to my mama's house with the help of his walking stick so that he could see this strange phenomenon with his own eyes. In the old days, he had been the *dewan* of Neelkuthi and had seen the many horses, *tumtums*, and the variety of guns that were owned by the sahibs, but he had never seen or heard of a device that could sing! Coming forward, he said in a voice querulous with age, 'Baba Hari, what did you say the name of this device was?'

'Gramophone,' said Hari Dadamoshai.

'And what does that mean?' Ramtaran Chakraborty asked.

'It means...it means...the song of the device,' offered Hari Dadamoshai after a little hesitation.

Ramtaran Chakraborty left for his heavenly abode when I was still very young. Consequently, other than the 'device that sings', he hadn't managed to see any of the other amazing creations of the modern world.

Now, that very house of Anadi Mama is lying in a state of disrepair and has been taken over by wild weeds. The door is all but broken; the window panels of the room on the first floor hang loose and swing to and fro in the wind. A banyan tree has managed to grow right on top of the roof, large enough for a goatherd to sit beneath it and play the flute. Anadi Mama is now an old man and stays in Kashi. He has two sons; one works at Jaunpur, another at Allahabad. They probably don't even mention the name of their distant ancestral village.

The house of Ramtaran Chakraborty—whom I spoke of earlier—a massive two-storey structure and the *daalan* that was used for puja now lie desolate and neglected. Bats large and small have made their nests near the latch at the top of the door; the broken-down floor houses the nest of cobras. Due to the fear of snakes, no one ventures close to these abandoned houses anymore. A few unfortunate individuals belonging to the lower, impoverished castes of the village have even lost their lives as a result of snake-bite when carelessly walking through such places.

Boro Mama's house is also in a similar ruinous condition.

Boro Mama used to work somewhere in the West. He was known in the village as a man of varied interests. He happens to be the cousin of my maternal uncles. Once during the monsoons when their part of the house caved in, Boro Mama's own paternal uncle had made fun of Boro Mama's family and had clapped and laughed at their misfortune. 'Their portion of the house has collapsed—serves them right! Now let me see where they go and put themselves up!' is what he had said with evident mirth and elation.

Boro Mama, at that time, was a young man of twenty-two, fatherless, and with his immediate family in dire straits. That paternal uncle had subsequently broken off all relations with them and left them to fend for themselves.

Boro Mama was never able to forget the events of that day and the insults that he had endured. It was due to this that while working in Rangoon, he had with great difficulty managed to save up a sum of five thousand rupees, which he eventually used to build the house that now stands in front of me. When this house was built, my mother wasn't yet married. Five thousand rupees of those times must be equivalent to at least sixty thousand rupees today.

That house is now lying neglected and has become the haunt of ghosts. It has probably been thirty years or so since a human being last set foot inside the house. The roof is overgrown with a jungle of thorny shrubs. Fig trees of all kinds have crowded together for want of space. Nobody ever comes to the house. Of Boro Mama's sons, one lives in Calcutta and another in Assam.

And that paternal uncle of Boro Mama's who had clapped and laughed at their calamity, even his mammoth house seems to have been entirely invaded by the jungle. Large locks and padlocks of ancient make can still be seen hanging on the doors. Although the locks are still there, the door panels have come loose and can be seen hanging, with only the chain to act as a fulcrum and support. From the open broken window of the first floor, a pot and a pitcher decorated by *Didu*'s own hands can be seen adorning the top of the cupboard—they have been lying there in that house these past forty years and more. It is also forty years since Didu passed away.

Dadu had only one son, Ramlal, a fine fellow. I can only recall an indistinct image of him now. He used to work in Darjeeling. Seven years after Dadu passed away, a telegram came from Darjeeling one day, to inform us of the son's death. I was only eleven then.

I clearly remember the events of that day.

I even remember that my own granny was cooking lentils that day. It was noon when the news came. She put the cooking aside and rushed to their house. I too accompanied her.

A heart-rending sight awaited us there. It is because of what we witnessed there that I remember the day so distinctly.

We saw Ramlal Mama's beautiful young wife standing in the verandah. She was well-known for her beauty in those parts. The verandah was already full of people who had come to express their sympathy at the tragic event. She was standing there in the midst of all those people. Someone was supposed to take her to the Ganga to help her bathe, to break the *shankha* that adorned her wrists and to wipe away the vermillion from her forehead. But no one seemed willing to take on this responsibility. Everybody was distressed and in tears. Only she wasn't crying—she was standing motionless, rooted to the spot. Shock seemed to have turned her body to wood. This is the image I can recall even today.

My grandma went and picked up Ramlal Mama's baby boy from the porch. A few days later, the child's mother took him with her and went away to her parents' place. I don't know whether she ever returned to her husband's home. I've heard that the boy is a grown man now and works somewhere in the West.

After wandering for a while in the midst of that jungle, I'd just returned to where I'd left the main path when I noticed Pareshnath coming down the road. Pareshnath is a distant maternal uncle of mine, but not much older than me. Then how come he has aged so much, I wondered.

When he came closer, I accosted him and said, 'Mama! Do you recognise me? How are you?'

Pareshnath looked at me mouth agape, and said, 'I seem to have seen you somewhere. Your face looks so familiar.'

I laughed and said, 'Excellent! I'm Kanai, Sitanath Chakraborty's nephew!'

In a flat voice he said, 'Oh.' That was all.

And yet, the two of us had been childhood playmates. I saw no sign of enthusiasm or joy on his face on seeing a childhood friend after so many years. He seemed to have become peculiar.

I asked him, 'Are you all right?'

There actually seemed no need to put that question to him, but I had to, for the sake of propriety.

'What can I say? I am waiting for death to bring me succour,' he replied.

Having said this, he was about to leave, but I stopped him and said, 'Please wait. Do you recognise me?'

'Yes, you are Kanai.'

'Are you distressed because of any illness?' I asked.

'I suffer from asthma,' he replied.

'I see. And are you receiving any treatment?'

'I will receive it by the Ganges when I lie down on the funeral pyre. I barely get to eat, and you're talking of treatment and medicines.'

'Okay, tell me, are any folks from our time still living in this *para*?'

'There's *Boro Jaethima*. She lives all alone.'

The lady Pareshnath referred to as Boro Jaethima is Dadu's (Ramlal's father) second wife. I remembered her from the days when I was a child. Even back then she had been an old lady. So she was still alive? She was the one who had brought up Ramlal Mama after his mother passed away. I remember that when Ramlal Mama died, she had already attained a considerable age. I distinctly remember how overcome with grief she had been at the news of Ramlal's sudden death, how she had wept and cried loudly and was inconsolable. She must be at least eighty-two or eighty-three now, no less.

I went to meet her.

Making my way with difficulty through the dense undergrowth, I managed to enter the huge house. Someone seemed to have cleared and maintained a very narrow path leading towards the house.

The moon was bright. From within the precincts of Nobo Moira's house, where our primary school classes used to be held, the howling of a jackal could be heard.

On entering the house, I noticed a decrepit old woman with a stoop holding an earthen lamp in her hand. Having offered evening prayers to the *tulsi* plant, she was stepping over the undergrowth of *kalmegh* on the cracked verandah and making her way very slowly towards the entrance of the house.

'Grandma!' I called.

'Who is it?' asked the old lady as she turned to look around. She couldn't recognise me. Of course, it wasn't possible for her to do so after all these years!

'Who are you?'

'I'm Kanai, Sitanath Chakraborty's nephew.'

The old lady stopped in her tracks as if taken by surprise and peered into my face. Compared to Pareshnath, her reaction and the expression on her face were more animated. The life-force hadn't left her yet, I thought.

'Oh! You're that little son of Satyabhama's! How grown-up you are now! Come, come into the verandah and sit down,' she invited me in.

The old lady went into the house to put away the earthen lamp, came back and sat near me. I asked her, 'Grandma, how long have you been living alone in this house?'

'For an eternity!' she said. 'Ever since *he* died.' She was referring to her husband.

'I see. Didn't you have any children of your own, Grandma?'

'I had a baby girl, but she died at the age of nine months. After that, I brought up that infant boy.'

'Who are you referring to?'

'His name was Ramlal.'

'I understand,' I said. 'I remember that he passed away when I was still a child.'

Grandma gave a long sigh and said, 'There's no one now, *Babu*. I don't even remember how long back it was when I came to this house as a bride. Seems like a distant memory. I was married off at the age of nine. The co-wife of the house, Ramlal's mother, was around eighteen or nineteen years old then. Subsequently, Ramlal was born. What need did I have to care for him? Yet, I took care of him and brought him up with my own hands. His mother didn't take any responsibility for him.'

'What would your age be now, Grandma?'

'It must be more than four times twenty.'

'And for how long have you been living in this house alone?'

'As I told you, Babu, I haven't left this house since he passed away. It was around the time when Ramlal had taken up a job. Ramlal's wife used to stay here in the house with me. After Ramlal's death, *Bouma* left this place.'

'Did she ever come back?'

'No. Bouma's father's home was in Calcutta. A city girl. What would she come back here for?!'

'Did she have a baby boy?' I asked.

Grandma looked at me with a surprised expression and said, 'How do you know of this?'

'Just a childhood memory. Where is that boy now?'

'I don't really know. I'd heard that he works somewhere in the West.'

'Do they write to you?'

'No.'

'Is Ramlal Mama's wife still alive?'

'There is really no way for me to know about that, Babu.'

'Did she never inquire about your well-being?'

'Why would she do so, Babu? After all this time. They hardly have anything to do with me anymore. As you know, in terms of our relationship, Bouma is actually my co-wife's daughter-in-law. What sympathy can she possibly have for me? As for *Khoka*, he won't have any recollection of me. He was only a year and a half old when they went away. I stay alone here. I can hardly recall since when I've been here. It has been such a long, long time. I don't have anyone anymore.'

'Does anyone from your parents' place or family keep in touch?'

'My parents' place is in Moshaat village near Hooghly. Those parts have been devastated by malaria. I had a brother who used to run a shop in Tarakeshwar. Since my husband died, my brother has never enquired about me or my well-being. I can't even say whether he is still alive or not.'

Then getting up, she said, 'You sit here, Babu. I'll be right back.'

Grandma went into the house and started rummaging for pots and utensils to prepare something for me to eat. These ancient houses tend to have compact doors and windows and are therefore somewhat dark even during the daytime. And in the evening too, the huge house remains dark because there is a shortage of oil for the lanterns. Grandma uses only two or three rooms. The rest of the house serves as a nest for all kinds of bats!

After a while she reappeared with a bamboo tray, on which there was some parched rice and coconut *laddoo*s, and keeping it in front of me, she said, 'Here's something for you!'

'What was the need for all this, Grandma?' I protested.

'You're Satyabhama's son, and you've come here after such a long time. How can I allow you to return without offering you anything? I would have loved to prepare something nice for you; it's just that I don't have very much myself.' Grandma's voice became heavy with emotion as she said this. Then she asked, 'Will you have some green chillies with this? Shall I pick some for you?'

'No, Grandma, I don't eat chillies.'

'Tell me son, those kings who had filed cases and counter-cases against each other...is all that settled now?'

'What cases are you speaking of? And between which kings?' I asked.

'That I cannot say. But everybody used to talk about it. At that time, rice had become scarce, there were no clothes to be bought, and even kerosene was not available. People used to say that there was a court case or something like that, between some kings. Is all that over now?'

I realised that she was referring to the Second World War. I said, 'Yes, Grandma, that has ended. Quite a long time back.' Then I continued, 'Tell me something...'

'Yes, Babu?'

'Do you know that our country has gained independence?'

'Gained what?'

'Independence. Meaning, as a nation, we're not subservient to any foreign power anymore. The British have left the country.'

'You mean the Queen's reign is no more?'

Queen, indeed! I thought it better not to worry her with any political complexities. To change the course of the conversation, I asked, 'How do you manage to fend for yourself, Grandma?'

'I have two-three *bighas* of land on which paddy is cultivated. We are *zamindars*, and our family has owned the land for a long time. The tenants who farm the land are good people, and I get my little share of paddy from them and some rent as well. I have to make do with that,' she explained.

I had finished eating the parched rice and laddoos. Grandma brought some water for me in a *ghoti*.

Grandma sighed deeply and said, 'I still see Ramlal, as he was when he was a ten-month-old Khoka. A cuddly baby with big eyes, crawling all over the place. I see my little *Khuki*. I see Ramlal's baby boy. It's as if the past events of yesteryears replay themselves in front of my eyes. Ramlal hasn't forgotten me even today—he used to love me a lot. He would say to me, "*Chhoto Ma*, I'll come someday and take you and your daughter-in-law away with me to the place where I work." Some mountainous region it was. It's very cold out there, I am told.'

Startled by a sudden noise, I said, 'What is that?'

Grandma laughed toothlessly and said, 'Did you get a fright? That is the sound of bats squeaking in the rooms. These are everyday occurrences. I've got used to all this now. And that is not all. There are enormous snakes in the house. They all consider this as their dwelling place. But they don't cause any harm. Sometimes when I'm lying on my bed, I can feel them crawl over my body and then go their way,' she said, calmly.

Shocked out of my wits, I exclaimed, 'You don't say!'

'I see them as well. Many times. At other times, in the dark of the night, they feel like ice on the body. It is then that I become aware of their presence.'

She continued with a sigh, 'What should I say, Babu? It's all destiny. Why else would a golden boy like Ramlal leave me all of a sudden? Nobody could say that he was my co-wife's son. Even a son born of a woman's own womb could not love her as much as Ramlal loved me. After all, there is so much one gets to see all around these days. After his marriage, he brought his wife to me and said, "See! I've brought along a *dasi* to take care of you." I replied, "Don't say that, son. Why would she be my dasi? She is the Lakshmi of the house." He laughed and said, "No, Mother, who else could be the household Lakshmi when you yourself are there for us?" I remember it all so clearly. It was a long day in the month of *Asharh* when, bringing my daughter-in-law along, my Khoka stood on the *peeri* with milk and *alta*.'

Saying this, Grandma broke down. I tried to comfort the old lady, knowing all along that it was of no avail.

I should be leaving now, I thought. As long as I stay, she will continue to speak of Ramlal. Clearly, she hasn't had anyone to listen to her all this while. Who can say how long it has been since she was able to pour her heart out to someone?

Wiping her tears, she said, 'Still, I go on. My husband left me long back, but every day at dawn, I offer the earthen lamp with my prayers in his home and console myself by performing this essential duty. Ideally, my grand-daughter-in-law should have been doing all this today—offering the earthen lamp, blowing the conch shell...' she trailed off.

I touched Grandma's feet to seek her blessings and took my leave of her.

An owl cried out in the jungle near the Durga *mandap*. In the moonlight, this ancient edifice amidst the thick undergrowth of kalmegh presented a mysterious and eerie appearance. It has been witness to the history of so many ages.

I turned around to look. Grandma had come to the edge of the verandah and was standing there, looking down the path at my receding figure.

How long will you remain a captive of this brick-and-mortar prison, Grandma? Who can say how long it will be before this Ahalya turned-to-stone will find her deliverance?

Previously published in Bengali as '*Boro Didima*' in *Bibhutibhushan Golpo Shomogro*.

A Mystery

I'd heard this story from a friend of mine. He is presently a professor in a college in Calcutta. He is an intelligent man, not easily swayed by any particular sentiment or belief. Even though he is not terribly materialistic, he has an inclination to experience and enjoy life, and he has the necessary ability to do so as well.

That night it was raining heavily. Over cups of hot tea and the customary accompaniments, we chatted pleasantly about different things, and of course, we shared anecdotes about ghosts. My friend is a professor of science. He told us a story which I found both interesting and astonishing. I suppose it can be said that coming from him, the story has a certain value and authenticity to it. So let the story be told in his own words.

I was appearing for my BA examinations. After the Honours exams were done, we were given a leave of four or five days. After all these years I don't quite remember what occasioned the leave. There was a friend of mine named Bhabataran Ghoshal. His house was in Belghere. Bhabataran used to chew betel leaves in the class and smoke a lot of cigarettes when he was outside the class. He enjoyed indecent, bawdy conversations and narrating tall tales; there was no end to his craftiness. We used to get along well, the reason being that back then I myself was quite a wily character. Now when I think of those times, I feel amused. Anyway, to come back to what I was saying.

The day the Honours exams ended, Bhabataran insisted on taking me along to his house. We took the train. After we got off, we had to walk quite a long distance from the station because his house was located almost on the banks of the Ganges. At some point during my stay at his house, we got into an argument. I can't remember what it was about, but the altercation took such an unpleasant turn that we almost came to blows. Oh, the days gone by! Bright sunshine one moment, and cloudy skies the next. That was how it was wont to be back then.

In any case, feeling extremely vexed, I left his house late in the evening. Being subjected to such behaviour, how could a gentleman stay on?

Taking the Barrackpore Trunk Road that goes towards Calcutta, I started walking at a brisk pace. It was a bright, moonlit night. There was hardly anyone on the road. Occasionally, a few motor vehicles could be seen, and except for a drunk coolie, I didn't come across any other human being.

Suddenly I felt that it wouldn't be possible to walk the entire stretch at one go. I needed some rest. I kept looking out for a place as I walked, and after a while, I came across a house with a garden and entered its precincts. From the look of the house, it seemed to me that it wasn't inhabited. At the most, there might be a gardener or a caretaker, and he might allow me to sit in the garden if I gave him a little money. There must be a pond in the garden, with paving around its edges. On this moonlit summer night, I thought I could get lucky and enjoy a bit of rest by its side.

When I entered the garden, it was evident that no one stayed in the house, nor did people visit it frequently. Cogon grass of over a hand's length grew in the paths of red gravel, and there were beds of flowering plants and wild weeds of all kinds. As I moved further into the garden and looked around, I could see that the house belonged to a well-to-do person, or at least, at the time that it was built, the owner had been very well off. Every plant that grew in the garden and every stone and brick used to build the house reflected good taste. At various spots in the garden half-concealed by the wild weeds and flowering plants, I noticed some stone sculptures of celestial nymphs. Many of them had lost a limb or had chipped noses. Some of the statues stood with faces pointing towards me, while others had their backs to me. I went a little ahead and saw a path going to the left. I took it and found that it ended at a pond. But the pond wasn't of the kind I'd expected to find. It was clearly built in days long gone. Huge cracks had appeared on the bottom, and banyan trees had taken root on either side. The pond had been surrounded by a paved border at some point in the past, but the steps that led down to it had crumbled in several places. The fear of snakes at night didn't let me approach it anyway.

There was a bench at some distance from the steps and feeling weary and tired, I lay down on it. I didn't know when I fell asleep, but when I woke up, it was already quite late in the night. Glancing around, I felt a strange sense of misgiving.

My eyes first fell on the nymph-like statues that were positioned at some distance from the bench. I had the impression that all the while that I was sleeping, the statues were facing another side and were engaged in doing something, and that as soon as they observed that I was waking up, they had somehow managed to return to their earlier positions and now stood frozen as before in their original posture and manner.

Astonished, I sat up on the bench and rubbed my eyes. Did I get this idea because I was sleepy? I didn't think so. Waking up from my sleep, I had distinctly seen that one of the statues was about to do something, when realising that I had woken up, it had desisted from carrying out its intention. My entire body felt torpid and numb. I hadn't slept well and didn't feel rested. I didn't feel like resuming my walk, so I lay down on the bench again. I had hardly lain down when I fell asleep again. But just before sleep overtook me, I could feel that my mind was still inquisitive. What was that statue about to do when it saw me waking up?

In the chilly air of the late night, I lay in deep sleep on that bench in the garden. When I woke up next, the moon was descending towards the west, and from behind the tall trees, it continued to cast its rays on the earth. The trees threw long shadows on the expanse of shrubs below.

I felt that whatever was in the garden when I'd first entered, it wasn't the same anymore. Some change had come over the place. This notion grew stronger as I moved from slumber to a state of wakefulness. And yet, I couldn't make out exactly what had changed and where. Suddenly my attention was drawn to the view directly in front of me. I rubbed my eyes. Yes, that was where something looked different. But what was it that had changed? I couldn't tell what it was. A minute or two passed. And then suddenly the truth dawned on me, and as it did, a current of lightning seemed to pass through my entire body, making me numb and dizzy.

Where had the statue of the nymph-like creature on that pedestal gone? The pedestal was empty now.

It didn't quite sink in at first. Was there really a statue on that pedestal before? Perhaps it had been somewhere else. Might it be that my sight and memory were mistaken?

But how was that possible? Who could have taken away such a large heavy stone statue in the dead of night? No, I must have been mistaken.

But it was that very statue I had noticed on coming awake the first time—it had turned to the other side and was about to do something. And it had been on the platform right in front of me. If it hadn't been there, how could I have possibly seen it while lying on the bench? I distinctly remembered that I had first become aware of it when I'd come to lie down on the bench. At that time, its side had been turned towards me. I also remember thinking, are statues of this kind imported from Italy? Or are they sculpted in our own country?

How could I have been mistaken on so many counts? But if it was not a fault of my perception or memory, then the question was: how could that figurine have disappeared? Who took it away in the middle of the night? Did a thief carry it off?

If that was the case, then how was it that in all those days when the garden was lying unguarded, no one had stolen the figurine, and it was only when a man, wholly alive, was lying on a bench right in front of it that a thief would take it into his head to carry it away?

No, that didn't seem plausible either.

I can't say why, but I began to feel afraid. My body started to shiver. Not much of the night remained. There really was no need for me to stay there anymore. I decided I should resume my walk towards Calcutta.

As soon as this thought occurred to me, I got up from the bench. I wanted to go to the pond to wash my face and hands before leaving, and I was about to make my way towards it when again, I stood transfixed.

Just below the *aamloki* tree that stood at the edge of the pond, there had been a statue. Where was it now? It had a broken hand and had hence drawn my attention. But inexplicably, right in front of me stood its empty pedestal.

A strong sense of doubt and misgiving took hold of me. I looked around the garden. There had been so many figurines dotting the garden amidst the dense undergrowth. Made of white stone, they had shone brightly in the moonlight. The moonlight still illuminated the garden, but where were all those nymph-like figurines? Not one was to be seen!

Were they all stolen in one night? Had the thieves been waiting for just this night to execute their task?

Astonishing! I stared all around like a fool. It was now that I finally understood. All this while I'd been wondering what had changed, what transformation had taken place. So this is what had happened across the length and breadth of the garden while I was sleeping.

By now, taking one step at a time, I'd almost reached the edge of the pond, when I happened to glance at the water in the pond, and I received the shock of my life. My entire body trembled with fear.

All the stone nymphs of the garden had entered the pond and were swimming in it. Yes! As clearly as one could see in the daytime, they were gliding in the water, swimming this way and that. But there was something else that I noticed. The figurines hadn't come alive. They were still in the form of statues, and yet they were swimming!'

At this point in the story, someone from our group interrupted my friend and asked, 'You saw this clearly?'

Looking at us, my friend said, 'Although many years have passed since that incident took place, I haven't forgotten the events of that night. Even today, I can distinctly see that scene as if it is in front of my eyes. In fact, I recall it from time to time. Of course, it's up to you whether you wish to believe me or not. I haven't ever asked anyone to trust in the veracity of the story.'

I asked him, 'Had you consumed cannabis while you were at your friend's place? Or some other intoxicant maybe?'

'I would never touch such things back then, nor do I do so now. You must trust me when I say this,' he replied.

All of us had been listening to his story with rapt attention. We asked eagerly, 'What happened next?'

My friend resumed his tale.

I stood there silently, my eyes riveted on the vision in front of me. I felt as if I'd turned mad or some severe illness had taken hold of me. What was I seeing? I still remember that there was a coconut or a palmyra tree near the wall on the western side of the garden. The moon was then hidden behind the branches of that tree. I remember that very well. I once again directed my gaze towards the pool and beheld the same astonishing and unnatural sight—those white marble figurines swimming and playing around, as if alive, in the depths of the pond! It made my head whirl. I began to doubt my sanity. My heart in my mouth, I scampered as fast as I could towards the entrance of the garden. When I reached it, I felt as if—of course, I cannot be entirely sure of this—but I felt as if a group of girls had suddenly broken into giggles and laughter. The next moment I found myself hurrying towards the Barrackpore Trunk Road and in a short while, I reached it.

I know what you will ask me now. Whether or not I ever went back to that place?

I went back there the very next day in fact. Not alone, but with three of my friends. When we arrived there, I saw the old, broken-down house with a garden that was overgrown with flowering plants, shrubs and weeds. A number of stone figurines on pedestals could be seen here and there, some with broken hands and a few with chipped noses. But there was no sign of anything abnormal or unnatural.

One of my friends suddenly called out to me. I found him next to the figurine that stood underneath the aamloki tree. A thorny creeper had grown upwards from the ground and had wrapped itself around the statue's feet. The creeper, which must have been at least a year old, may have grown during the previous monsoon. It was intact and entirely unbroken. That was the conclusion we drew after examining it closely.

And yet, I was dead sure that this figurine had also entered the water last night, and that I'd seen its empty pedestal with my own eyes. Why! I'd been standing right here, at this very spot next to the steps, for quite some time.

My friends said, 'In that case, how could the creeper be so untouched? The growth around the feet of the statue is at least a year old. It hasn't grown overnight!'

Their reasoning was irrefutable.

What answer could I possibly offer given that I too had started to mistrust myself?

Previously published in Bengali as '*Rohoshyo*' in *Bibhutibhushan Golpo Shomogro*.

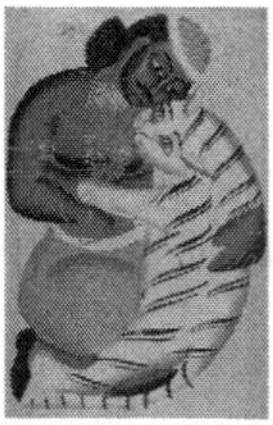

The Hunter

Magniram is a boy of the jungle. His parents had prayed to Lord Rama for a child, and that's how he came to be delivered into his mother's lap. His people are accustomed to showing humility before God as well as man, hence they do not give their children tasteless names like *Lakhpatiya* and *Daulatram* the way people of the merchant class sometimes tend to do.

Magniram's house is in Jhanpri-shol village.

On the motorable road (that passes at some distance from the village), there is a diversion on the left and a small narrow path leading straight ahead. Some way down this track one comes across the *shimul* plantation of the Forest Department—around a hundred and fifty to two hundred shimul trees on three or four acres of land. In the months of *Phalgun* and *Chaitra* when the shimul trees are in full bloom, what a marvellous sight it presents! The massive, leafless trees are aflame with the scarlet-red petals of the shimul flowers.

Crossing the stretch of shimul trees you come across a river called Borjor Nala. Huge rocks line the riverbank, and a dense growth of trees with overhanging shadows loom over them, forming a sylvan backdrop. And beneath the thick vegetation, the Borjor Nala, foaming and now swollen to twice its size with the water from the monsoon rains, rushes towards the distant Shoukh river. The Shoukh river, in turn, flows along the base of the Mahadal mountain range to meet the Mahanadi. Where the Mahanadi goes from there is not a matter the people of Jhanpri-shol concern themselves with. Across the Borjor Nala is the Chukurdi-Tukurdi Reserve Forest. Chukurdi is the name of a Christian village. In the middle of the village is a hut-like church built of thick, coarse *sabai* grass. The walls of the church are made of *sal* sticks. If you were to peek inside, you would see that a broken chair of tin is the only piece of furniture. This has been placed here for a pastor who comes from Bagodar once a month to have prayer sessions with the local people and read from the Holy Scripture.

Leaving Chukurdi village behind, if you go across a three-hundred-foot-high ridge of the Mahadal mountain range and cross an ancient *madar* tree, you will see nestled in the midst of the forest the Bonkati village. Only twenty-six families reside in this village. These are people of the *Munda* and *Kol* tribes, and not Christians.

Outside the precincts of the village, amid huge sal trees, is the shrine of Marang-Bonga or the Sun God. It is here that the people of Bonkati village offer the sacrifice of fowls to please the god. After the annual sacrificial ceremony, the villagers cook food together and have a communal meal. The pots used for the cooking are thereafter kept, as a custom, in a corner of the place of worship. Mounds of such pots, accumulated over the years, can now be seen.

After Bonkati village is Manganbera, and after that, Jhanpri-shol.

The purpose behind telling you all this is to help you understand how deep within the reserve forest Jhanpri-shol is situated.

If you stand in the middle of Jhanpri-shol and look around, you will see on the horizon the blue mountain range—comprising the Mahadal, Katchuri, Nankansbahal, Soychhuri and Chukurdi mountains—surrounding this small village on all four sides. The *jarul* flowers bloom during the monsoons, and the yellow flowers of the *kadam* tree, falling to the ground, form a bed of petals on the forest floor. The calls of hornbills can be clearly discerned, and musters of peacocks can be heard calling out in the higher reaches of the forest.

Magniram is a young boy of sixteen. His body has grown thin due to the onslaught of malaria. In these remote forest villages, when malaria once identifies a victim, it seems to put all its force into destroying the person! A majority of the people in this village, however, have elegant, healthy, well-proportioned physiques, looking much like sculptures carved out of stone. The girls are even more graceful and spontaneous, with faces expressing beauty as well as simplicity.

Magniram seems indifferent to everything these days. I can only attribute it to his state of ill health.

His friend Nankuya came to him and said, 'Come, let's go and catch some fish.'

With an irritated look, Magniram said, 'No, I won't go.'

'Why not?'

'My head feels dull and heavy.'

'Is it aching?'

'No, I just feel listless. How does it concern you anyway? I don't want to go. Get lost!'

'Why should I go? Huh?'

'Want me to set you right? Shall I?'

'You hardly have the strength to hold a handful of straw. How will you set me right? Think it is that easy?'

'Go away!'

'No, I won't.'

Provoked and angry, Magniram threw a stone at Nankuya. Laughing out loud, Nankuya ran off.

'Ran off' wouldn't be the right phrase. I should say he walked away. After all, who amongst them would possibly fear Magniram, worn out as he was from a severe bout of malaria!

This was also the cause of Magniram's sorrow—the reason why he was seen lying around sad and mirthless.

Borjor Nala takes a curve and passes close to Jhanpri-shol. It is about a mile away from the village, and lies just across a stretch of forest. During the monsoons, the people from the village go to the forest that lies across the Nala, to pick *kanda* potatoes. The creeper of this plant twines itself around the branches of the sal, *asan* and *arjun* trees and can climb to great heights in the mountains—to places where the peacocks are known to dance joyfully and perform their courtship rituals when the monsoon clouds gather on the mountain tops. And there its blue flowers bloom in all their glory.

The sight of those blue flowers fascinates Magniram, but because he cannot climb so high to collect them, the girls of the village mock and tease him mercilessly—consider him less than human in fact.

They say, 'Hey! He is but a weak boy. He is not made for such tasks.'

Magniram responds, 'It's not about the strength in my body. You girls just don't inspire the right kind of feeling and emotion.'

Budhni laughs and says, 'What do you have to do with our feelings?'

'It's not possible to explain such things to ignorant folks like you.'

'Hah! Listen to him refer to us as ignorant people! The fool thinks he is very learned.'

'Run along.'

'*You* run along!' the girls angrily respond. 'Do we sieve rice at your house or beat the corn there that we should go away?'

Now it's Magniram's turn to laugh. He finds it very funny when girls get angry. Clapping his hands in delight, he breaks into laughter.

He says, 'If you don't go, I'll hit you with sticks.' This angers the girls even more, and they start abusing him. He laughs and says, 'There's a rumble of thunder and a flash of lightning in the sky.'

Magniram breaks into a lovely song about the way lightning flares up in the sky, a song he has himself composed. The girls, their interest aroused, listen to him singing. The anger and loathing they feel for him abate considerably. During the Bonga festival, he teaches another one of his songs to his friend Nankuya and his little sister Ratu.

To tell the truth, Magniram is a poet at heart. It can even be said that he comes from a family of poets. His father is a *Santhal* but he lived in Ranchi for some time. It is in that distant city that he developed a devotion to Lord Rama, a religious belief he brought back with him to his home in the forest. That is also the reason why he has named his son Magniram; otherwise, a Santhal's son would never be so named.

Magniram's father is a well-known man in these parts. In Ranchi he has seen motor vehicles, *telephoonk*, electric fans, machines that sing songs—there is so much he has seen. It's been seventeen years now, but he still narrates those same old stories to the village folk. He thinks of the villagers with disdain and says, 'What have you seen of the world? You have never been anywhere outside this village. How will you be strong? When your mind is ignorant and lacks knowledge, how will it allow the body to be vigorous?'

Everyone comes to him to listen to his wondrous tales. They take his advice on various matters. Magniram rests in the light of his father's fame and hardly does any useful work. He only composes and sings songs. In such artistic matters, he is one step ahead of his father, the villagers say. But, of course, they say this with a sense of reproach and condemnation—not as praise.

Magniram's imagination carries him to the high reaches of the forest where the kanda creeper's beautiful blue flowers bloom. He feels great respect for his father and holds him in high esteem. His father has been to so many lands. How can the backward people of these parts understand what a great person he is!

If he had not been made weak through illness, Magniram, too, would have grown as a person and travelled far and wide by now. He had once gone to see the government's shimul plantation. A few days prior to his visit, government officials had come there to inspect the plantation. They'd left behind some sweets—strange red and green sweets wrapped in thin paper foil. He had initially wondered what they were. The plantation's watchman saw him and said, 'Those are sweets from the city. You can have them.'

Putting the sweets into his mouth, Magniram was amazed. He'd never eaten anything like that in his life. The government's sweets were indeed delicious.

He would have left behind everything and gone to those faraway places where such wonderful things exist. But that was not to be, because if he did go away, he would always tend to miss his father. Moreover, he is always unwell these days, due to which he is unable to climb trees, unable to cross the mountains to get to the dense forests of the higher reaches where the huge trees grow. But he wants to be a well-known person like his father and to make him happy.

Every year in the monsoons, herds of elephants come down from the hills to raid the *bajra* crops and destroy them. This year, too, the elephants came.

Officials from the *Ghatoyali* court notified the villagers that a huge rogue elephant had come down from the forests and was causing havoc and devastation in the villages. If someone could kill the rogue elephant, he would get a reward of a hundred rupees.

The group of young hunters in the village grew restless on hearing this news. But no one wanted to discuss the matter with another person, fearing that someone else would try and bag the reward.

A Santhal man named Deman came to Jhanpri-shol from Bonkati village and asked the villagers to gather together so he could address them.

He said, 'You won't be able to kill the elephant this year.'

The village people asked, 'Why do you say so?'

'This is a mad rogue elephant. You won't be able to kill it,' he repeated.

A young hunter said, 'You mean we won't be able to kill this elephant using a spear. So, you've come to teach us, have you? Isn't a rogue elephant an elephant?'

'Mark my words,' said Deman, 'this is not your regular elephant. This year at least two or three people will die from each *basti*. The officials from Ghatoyali court wouldn't have announced such a reward had it been easy to kill this elephant. You will see the truth of what I say.'

Deman is a hunter of repute in these parts. He has single-handedly killed a tiger using a spear and brought down elephants using poisoned arrows. There is not one person in these villages who will not take him at his word.

Magniram was present at the gathering. He looked at the strong, well-proportioned physique of the Santhal admiringly. What a man!

If he hadn't been made weak through illness, he too would have been strong today like Deman.

His father is now an old man. He, Magniram, will have to take over his father's responsibilities. He will have to take care of him and keep him comfortable and contented.

Magniram looks at the world with the eyes of a poet. All these thoughts going through his head of making his father happy are those of a mind vulnerable to the imagination. But the external world doesn't operate on imagination alone. It is also essential to learn the skills that may enable one to convert imagination into action. And that is where Magniram finds himself helpless.

For days on end, he sits alone and thinks about something. What he is thinking about, he alone knows.

His father will be a well-to-do man if he gets a hundred rupees, Magniram thinks. He will be able to buy a cow, and they will be able to drink the milk from the cow. They will also be able to buy some government sweets, like the ones he had eaten in the shimul plantation. Magniram can't even recall when his mother had passed away. His father had brought him up as his mother would have done. If he doesn't take care of his father now, who will?

That day he came to know that every night the rogue elephant came down to the banks of Nimpura and the Borjor Nala. Towards evening, without saying anything to anybody, Magniram went to the riverside.

The monsoon rains had increased the water level in the Borjor Nala. The water has broken through the riverbank and entered the fields of bajra on this side of the village. Since the opposite bank is flanked by the edge of the mountain, the water has been unable to ascend there and has instead turned about and overflowed the bank adjacent to the village. The fields of bajra bear the footprints of the elephant everywhere. Wherever it has stepped, it has destroyed the crops.

After many requests to Deman Santhal, Magniram has managed to collect two poisoned arrows from him. He has observed how a poisonous arrow can be shot at a target by blowing air through a bamboo blowgun. It is not an easy task as even those who shoot with practised hands hesitate and are afraid of missing the mark. As for Magniram, he is but a complete novice in this difficult art.

Even before dusk had fallen, Magniram climbed a *ber* tree on the edge of Borjor Nala and took his position. Lost in his thoughts, he kept singing softly to himself. He was hoping that the rogue elephant would come down from the jungles tonight.

Quite late in the night, the mad elephant indeed came down to the river. It wasn't an elephant but the devil himself! In fact, just before dusk today, it had killed an old man who was guarding the crops. His trunk still bore stains of fresh blood. Magniram grew agitated. The critical moment had arrived and with it, the opportunity to earn the reward of a hundred rupees for his father. Any unnecessary delay in action would be his failing.

Right at the moment when the elephant came close to the ber tree on the bank of Borjor Nala, Magniram took careful aim with the blowgun and blew into it with force. An arrow shot out in the moon-lit night.

The subsequent sequence of events was pieced together the next morning.

In the midst of the bajra plantation, at three separate places, were found the bloody, mangled remains of Magniram's body.

But Magniram's father was given a hundred rupees by the Ghatoyali court.

Let's see why this was so.

On the opposite side of the Borjor Nala, at the edge of the forest, the gigantic rogue elephant was lying dead. His body was discovered three days later. On either side of its trunk, close to the tusks, two arrows were found embedded. Taking a close look at them, the brave Santhal hunter Deman said, 'Hey! These are my arrows. Basudi's son had taken them from me the other day. How could I know that this is what he had in mind!'

It was because of Deman Santhal's testimony that the Ghatoyali court's Panikar Babu called Magniram's father to the court premises and, in front of four witnesses, took his thumb impression. Handing him ten notes of ten rupees each, he said, 'This is what a son should be like! Don't shed tears at his passing away. He wasn't just a son. The boy proved to be better than his father!'

Previously published in Bengali as '*Shikari*' in *Bibhutibhushan Golpo Shomogro*.

Illusion

Let me narrate to you the events that occurred two years back. I have a faint recollection. My mind seems to play tricks with me. How did I land up here? When I try to recall, I see myself walking on the path that leads from Bagula to Sidhrani.

I had a cook's job for many years, but have since lost it. Well, let the job go. I cannot say that I'm sad about it. What does make me sad however is that a misjudgment on the part of my employers led to the loss of my job. I hadn't stolen the *ghee*. I'm not even aware who stole it; and yet, as per the reasoning of the *babus*, it was I who was held guilty.

Shantipara, Sorshe, Bejerdanga. By the time I crossed them all, it was past noon. I was a young man, and I started feeling extremely hungry. Even though I had some money on my person, passing through these rural areas, till now I hadn't come across any eatery.

At one point along the road, I came across a lovely pond. I've always loved bathing in ponds. So, leaving my clothes at the broken edge of this one, I entered the water. I pushed aside the profusion of water hyacinths growing in the pond and immersed myself in the clear water. It was the end of the month of *Baishakh*, and it was already quite hot, so I was grateful for the bath. I washed the clothes I had been wearing and hung them to dry on the branches of a tamarind tree that was at some distance from the pond. My body was cooled by the bath, but my stomach was still burning with hunger. Are there no fruits growing in the forest at this time of year? I looked around but didn't find any.

At that moment I observed an old man coming towards the pond to have a bath. On seeing me, he asked, 'Where are you from?'

I said, 'I'm a poor Brahmin, wandering around in search of a job. For now, I'm extremely hungry. Where can I find some food? Can you tell me of someplace close by?'

The old man said, 'Wait a moment. Sit down. Let me have a bath. After that I will arrange everything.'

After finishing his bath, the old man took me along to his village. We entered an old house surrounded on all sides by plantations and jungles. He said, 'My name is Nibaron Chakraborty. This house belongs to me, but I don't stay here. My sons have a business in Calcutta. They live in Shyam Bazaar. This huge house lies vacant, while we stay in the city in a small house of three rooms. Such hardship! I come here once a month to keep the house in order. My sons do not want to come here. They fear the malaria that infests these villages. The back of this house has a large plantation with fruit-bearing trees of every possible variety, but there's no one to eat them, except ghosts. Will you stay here?'

'I could,' I said.

'What work do you do?'

'I'm a cook.'

'For the few days that I'm here, you may cook for the two of us.'

'Fine.'

My agreement to his proposition seemed to make the man happy. He immediately made arrangements for my food. After I'd eaten my fill, the old man gave me a mat and a thick pillow and said, 'You can take some rest now.'

Having walked since morning, I was exhausted and soon fell asleep. By the time I woke up the day had waned. Faint rays of the sun coloured the high branches of the trees. A jackal started calling in the jungle behind the house. I stepped out to take a stroll around the house and get a feel of the place. Wherever I looked, there were jungles of mango and jackfruit trees! There were no other houses to be seen. In the midst of the trees, I caught sight of a broken well. I peered inside it and saw that bats had made it their home.

Returning to the house, I found old Nibaron Chakraborty chewing tobacco. He asked me, 'Do you know how to make tea? Also, fry some parched rice. We'll mix it with some mustard oil and salt and have it with green chillies.'

Later, after dusk had fallen, he said, 'Put some rice to boil. There is some long-grained rice. You'll also find potatoes and some fresh ghee. We'll have *aloo bhat*.'

'As you say, sir!'

'You can make some *jhinge* curry for yourself. You will find the jhinge growing in the garden behind the kitchen. Take a lamp along, and pick some. And another thing. Always make sure there is some light when you are in the kitchen.'

'Of course! How can I possibly cook in the dark?'

'Exactly. That's what I meant.'

The house was indeed massive. Adding up all the rooms across the two storeys, there must have been at least fourteen or fifteen. And there was a huge verandah besides. Except for three or four rooms, all the others were locked. In front of the kitchen was a long porch, beyond which there were four or five coconut trees and a grapefruit tree. To pick the jhinges I would need to go into the yard beyond the porch and then take a turn to reach the area behind the kitchen. It wasn't completely dark yet, so I didn't carry a lamp as I went out.

Good god! What a dense jungle behind the kitchen! I found a wild jhinge vine laden with the vegetable. I started picking the young, green ones. Suddenly about ten hands away in front of me, and in the midst of the undergrowth, I saw a young woman, her face half-shrouded by the veil of a sari, bending down like me and picking jhinges. I strained my neck and looked at her twice, then turned around to gather some more of the vegetable for dinner. Before leaving, I looked at the woman again and saw that she was still picking jhinges.

Nibaron Chakraborty asked, 'Did you find the jhinges?'

'Yes sir, an abundance. Another person was also picking them.'

Surprised, he asked, 'Where?'

'In the stretch behind the kitchen. Towards the jungle.'

'Was it a man?'

'No, a lady.'

Nibaron Chakraborty's face assumed a strange, dissatisfied expression. He said, 'Where did you see the woman? Let's go and look.'

Accompanying him to the back of the kitchen, I saw that she was no longer there.

Nibaron said, 'Well, where's the woman?'

'She was there in that undergrowth.'

'Huh! What senseless things you say! Come, let's go. Seeing a woman here at this time of the day!'

I felt a bit astonished. If a woman from the village had come to pick a few wild jhinges, what was so unusual about it? I couldn't understand why Nibaron Chakraborty got so worked up! Moreover, although he was at the house today, once he returned to Calcutta, who would stand guard over his wild jhinges?

After dinner, the old man again brought up the topic of jhinges being stolen from the garden. He said, 'Why didn't you take a lamp along when you went to pick the jhinges? I'd asked you to keep a light handy, remember? Why didn't you do so?'

I couldn't understand why the old man was making such a fuss about the lamp. He seemed quite irritable. When I was able to see everything clearly—even discern a woman picking jhinges in the jungle—then what was the need for me to have taken a lamp along?

The old man continued, 'Once the evening fades, you must keep a light handy.'

'But why?'

'Please do as I say.'

Then he asked, 'How old are you?'

'Thirty-seven. Nearly thirty-eight.'

'You're much younger and less experienced than me. I'm sixty-three now. Therefore, listen and follow the instructions I give you.'

'Certainly, sir. I will do so.'

Late in the night, when I was deep in sleep, my slumber was broken by a noise in the room upstairs. It sounded like things were being moved about in the room, as if someone was shifting heavy boxes or furniture from one place to another. The old man was leaving for Calcutta the next morning. I guess he was re-arranging a few things before he left. But why so late in the night? Such a whimsical fellow!

In the morning, when I asked the old man about it, he looked confounded, and said, 'Me?'

'Yes, very late in the night.'

'Oh! Err...yes, that's right.'

'You could've asked me. I would have moved the things for you.'

Chakraborty *Moshai* didn't say anything. Before it was nine, I had prepared rice and lentils, and some jhinge fry. The old man ate his meal and tying up his bundle, left for Calcutta.

Before he left, he told me several times to look after the house and assured me that I would be quite comfortable staying there. He said, 'Son, take care of the house as you would your own, and stay in comfort. There are guavas in the plantation, mangoes and jackfruit as well, the best varieties of papaya, and many kinds of vegetables. There are three *bigha*s of cultivable land. The homestead itself is spread over one and a half bighas. In the absence of people to take care of the place, the plantation has been lying neglected, and the jungle has taken over. You can work hard, grow vegetables, eat your fill, and sell the rest. Think of it as your own house. Take care of the place and stay here in comfort,' he said again. 'There is nothing to worry about.' Then he said, 'There is something else I must tell you.'

'Yes, please tell me.'

Without any apparent reason, Chakraborty Moshai's tone became sour and he said, 'Many people will say a lot of things to you and put you in a bad humour, but don't lend your ears to what they say. Just take care of the house, stay here in comfort at your own sweet will, and don't listen to the idle talk of the villagers. The fruits and vegetables from the plantation will suffice as your food. I'm keeping two rooms open for your use.'

Then the old man left. I felt elated, as though he had suddenly raised me to the skies. Two spacious rooms in this colossal house were at my sole disposal. Besides, the enormous verandah, the kitchen and the porch were there for me to use. The house had a well of its own, so there would be no water problems. There was ample firewood, so cooking and heating water would not be an issue either. I had been given an advance of ten rupees, there was long-grained rice in stock and the trees were loaded with mangoes and jackfruit. It felt like God's own bounty had suddenly landed in my lap!

Towards evening I went in search of a grocer's shop to buy some oil and salt. Oh my! There is such a dense cover of jungles and plantations in this village. Are there no human habitations at all close to the Chakrabortys' house? I'd walked half a mile along a narrow path in the jungle when I met a man. I saw that he had an empty oil can in his hand and realised that he also was on his way to obtain some oil. On seeing me, he asked, 'Where do you stay?'

'At Nibaron Chakraborty's residence.'

'Nibaron Chakraborty's house? How come?'

'I look after the place. I arrived yesterday.'

'You won't be able to stay at that house.'

'Why not?

'I've said what I had to say. You'll see. So many people have come to stay at that house and left. The Chakrabortys themselves are unable to stay there, what to say of other folks? The sons and daughters-in-law of the family don't come there ever.'

'Why is that?'

'How would I know?! But that is a frightful house. You're new to these parts. Be extremely cautious.' Without saying anything more, the man left.

I located a grocer's shop, made my purchases, and then returned to the house. By then the evening was fading and dusk about to fall. Looking at that huge, ancient, two-storeyed house standing in the middle of the jungle, my heart skipped a beat. The house had such a an eerie appearance, like an animated being with hands outstretched, advancing towards me to devour my puny self! Why did it look so terrifying?

No, it's nothing. The man I had met on the jungle path is responsible for my low spirits. When I'd left the house to buy groceries, I'd been feeling quite merry. This sudden downswing in my mood is a result of the conversation with that man who had tried to instill fear in my heart. What was the need to go out of your way to do me good, Babu? Did I ask for it? Old man Chakraborty has already told me that people will say such things, and that I should not pay them any attention.

You think I can't make out the reason behind this idle talk? The villagers obviously love to lay their hands on the fruits and vegetables that grow in the plantation. If there is a dedicated attendant in the house, they'll be unable to do so; hence it would be in their best interests to drive away any caretaker of the house. Didn't I see that woman stealing jhinges from the plantation just last evening?

I haven't stayed in such comfort for a long time. Nor have I ever had an opportunity to earn money without putting in too much hard work. I only needed to cook two meals for myself every day, and that was it!

I had finished the cooking in the morning, so I sat down on the porch, and feeling relaxed, started singing to myself. I felt I was the lone master of this large abode. There was no one to say anything to me or ask me for anything. I could do just as I pleased.

I was lost in such thoughts when all of a sudden I was startled out of my reverie! From the mouth of the duct that runs down from the first storey, water began to flow in a steady stream as if someone were washing their hands and feet in the verandah there. I immediately got up, and standing at the edge of the porch, looked up to see what was going on. The water continued to flow steadily. A flight of stairs led to the first floor. The door leading to the staircase was locked, and Chakraborty Moshai had taken away the keys. So there was no way I could go up to the first storey. But where was the water coming from?

After ten minutes or so, the flow of water suddenly stopped. I thought perhaps Chakraborty Moshai had stored some water in an earthen pot or vessel, which had somehow overturned. That must be it. Otherwise, where else could the water have come from?

Sometime later, I decided to retire for the night. As soon as I put off the lights and lay down, I fell asleep. Quite late in the night,

I was roused from my sleep to see moonlight coming through the window and falling on my bed. The fragrance of some flower was also drifting in, the perfume quite enchanting.

What flower could it be?

Half-asleep, I was thinking that I hadn't seen any sweet-smelling flower in the vicinity of the house.

Suddenly I jumped up from the bed. Who was that? A woman, crossing the porch, went past the window. I saw her clearly. There could not be any mistake. I got up instantly, opened the door and went and stood on the porch. As I stood there, two things became clear. First, the fragrance was dense on the porch as if during her short presence there the woman had left her perfume lingering in the air. And second, this wasn't the fragrance of some flower. But what it was, I couldn't quite tell.

I felt a strange sensation, almost like I was intoxicated! Why have I come out? Oh yes, I saw a woman crossing the porch a while ago, the one who has spread this intense fragrance. But I can't see her anymore. Where has she gone?

After a while, I returned to my room and went back to sleep. That's how the events of that night ended.

When I woke up in the morning, it all seemed like a dream. I felt quite light-hearted as I went about the tasks of the day. I thought about how I would clear the dense undergrowth and thick cover of shrubs, and grow a great quantity of vegetables. I started deliberating on this and other such things.

However, there is one inconvenience of staying in this place. It is a very solitary existence. Even if there was one person close by with whom I could converse, things wouldn't be so bad—but there is no one I can talk to. This is troubling and a matter of great anguish.

That afternoon an incident took place.

I was just taking the rice off the stove when I heard something strange, as if several people were laughing together on the verandah of the first storey. It wasn't a giggling kind of laughter but a terrible roaring sound that made my body tremble. The skies seemed to shake and the air ring with that frightful laughter.

Flinging the pot of rice aside, I ran out of the room. Going to the porch, I looked up towards the first floor but saw nothing. The laughter had died down by then. The windows on the ground floor were closed. Those on the first storey were also fastened.

What is going on? Has a gang of villainous people established themselves on the first floor? Going to the entrance of the stairs that lead to the first storey, I found that the lock was still hanging untouched.

I wasn't really afraid yet, the reason being that it was daytime and there was bright sunshine all around. At this time of the day, one's mind doesn't have an intuition of ghosts. If I'd heard the same laughter at nighttime, I would have probably become unconscious with fear and my jaws locked shut so that keys would have been required to open my mouth!

Returning to the kitchen, I set some jhinge curry to cook on the stove. Jhinges are plentiful in the plantation and I can pick as many as I want. It's my house. All the creepers and trees are mine. Ah, the intoxication of being a house owner! Only since yesterday have I been experiencing it. Something like this has never before occurred in the life of this poor Brahmin.

I remained alert for any more sounds from the rooms upstairs but I couldn't even hear a pin drop. After having my meals, I lay down on my bed and went to sleep. In the depths of my slumber, I distinctly heard the laughter and conversation of many people inside the room. It was as if I was in a marriage hall full of people, and I'd fallen asleep in a corner, but still, in my sleep, I was able to hear the sound of their voices! Maybe my mind was playing tricks on me. Or maybe it was the state of mind I was in after hearing the laughter coming from the second storey that had caused this!

Thereafter, nine days passed without incident.

It is an acquired habit of a man's mind that it wants to forget unpleasant events as fast as it can, and is able to do so. I tried to convince myself that nothing unnatural had occurred, that whatever had happened were mere illusions created by my mind. Seeing a woman in this uninhabited place was the fault of my eyes; hearing human laughter was the fault of my ears! It was all nothing but a huge mistake.

In these nine days, my body and mind have recovered and I am back to my original state. I eat my fill and spend most of the time sleeping. There is no work that I'm expected to do, so a kind of laziness has taken hold of me. By nature, I'm a hard-working person who doesn't like to lie around doing nothing, but owing to excessive labour in the past many months, a kind of fatigue has set in. I therefore only feel like resting.

Towards evening I thought of clearing some of the jungle behind the kitchen, of course, without hurting the jhinge creepers, and plant seeds of other vegetables there. Also, I'd noticed an ash gourd creeper had taken root in the middle of the jungle. I would use a bamboo stick and direct it towards the roof of the kitchen. One feels happy to work in this house, the reason being that spade, sickle, weeding hook, crowbar, axe—everything that one needs for farm work—is kept ready in a corner.

I'd hardly worked for half an hour or so when I noticed that the woman I'd seen on the first day was there again, and bending low in the undergrowth she was busy picking jhinges.

Simultaneously from the rooms on the second storey there was a huge clamour. It sounded like many voices, around fifty or so, were all making a noise together. And thereafter, there was a loud bang. The sound seemed to suggest that all the doors and windows of the house had suddenly flown open as if struck by a storm.

Throwing the implements on the ground, I looked upwards. I went and stood on the porch towards the front of the house. But no, not a single window nor any of the door panels on the first storey had opened! Everything was just as it was supposed to be.

Did the house occasionally suffer from fits? Why did such horrid screams emanate from it now and then? This time around there could be no mistake—engaged in my work, in an entirely healthy state of mind, I'd heard the screams and the noise just moments ago. Now, once again, there was absolutely nothing to be heard. Only silence all around.

And amid all this commotion, that woman had come to pick jhinges. I darted to the back of the kitchen. But there was no one there.

That night an incident took place—quite a funny incident actually.

After dinner, I lay down to sleep. Drowsiness had just begun to overcome me, when suddenly I heard a sound and was awake again. Looking around, I saw that several people had gathered around my bed, all of them wearing red turbans and carrying small sticks in their hands. The surprising thing was that all of them looked identical. It seemed like the same person had been multiplied fifty times and more, or countless mirrors were reflecting the same face. That's how it appeared at first.

A voice said, 'There is someone who has come in our midst today.'

Another voice answered, 'A mortal man has made this place his abode. I haven't seen the house, but I have heard. Those who know how to see, I've heard them say. There is a person staying in that house.'

'That's all a lie! Where's the house?'

'None of us have seen it.'

'Then come, let's start our jig.'

The dance of the ghosts! I had only heard about it till then. But now I was seeing it with my own eyes. Good God! How strange it was. Beating their sticks on the ground, the group of people started a formidable dance—a veritable *tandav* of sorts. Innumerable times they passed right through my body and back! And all this to the accompaniment of terrible, monstrous shouts and cries.

They didn't touch my bed or any part of me. It was as if they were not even aware of my presence there. Subjected to the roar of their shouts and their Bhairav dance, I lost sensibility.

When I regained consciousness, I saw the moonlight of the last phase of night entering the room through the window and falling on my bed. In the cool air of the room, I could smell that sweet fragrance of flowers. In a half-conscious state, I gazed through the open window at the trees and branches shining in the half-moon light.

I can't say how much later the day finally dawned, but when I got up from bed, I felt rested and alive with the good health and freshness that one feels after a good night's rest. I didn't 'feel' as if my sleep had been interrupted.

Then who was it that had witnessed the dance of the ghosts? Was it all just a creation of my mind then, a dream?

If that's all it was, then how could I explain the sweet fragrance that had filled the room during the last phase of the night? Where did that come from? It is only when the woman walks by the house that this distinctive sweet smell spreads through the air. The fragrance cannot be a creation of my mind. Even now, I can feel it in my nostrils. It must be the fragrance of some unknown forest flower. Yes, that's what it must be.

Later, when I had gone to the shop to buy some oil, the grocer greeted me, and then he asked, 'I say, do you see something?'

'No.'

'Do you hear sounds?'

'No.'

'You seem to be a saintly person. Do you know any Tantric practices? Some *mantras* to keep away spirits, maybe?'

'Give me the oil and let me leave. All that stuff is nonsense.'

'Okay, tell me, haven't you seen a woman in that house? And a smell...?'

'What kind of smell?'

'Like the fragrance of some flower.'

'No.'

'You should count yourself lucky. Whoever has stayed there has said that they often used to see a woman. Subsequently, they would refuse to leave the place and then, progressively becoming weak and emaciated, they would finally die. Two men have suffered this fate so far. That house is the haunt of ghosts. They turn people mad. Those who stay there lose their mind. They fall so much in love with the place that they stop eating and taking care of themselves. They just lie around the house, not wanting to leave it. But you seem to be well-versed in the mantras that can keep ghosts away. We folks never dare to go anywhere close to that house. It can make a sane man insane.

I bought the oil and turned homewards. On my way back I began to wonder if I had started to lose my mind.

But I'd hardly entered the house when I felt that I was thinking on the wrong lines. I'm extremely happy here, I thought. Where else would I go? I'm fine and doing well. Doing mighty well in fact!

It's been two years since the events I've just narrated and two years since I've been lying around in this house. Chakraborty Moshai doesn't give me a salary, but that hardly bothers me. I take care of the house, sell the produce from the plantation, and watch them dance day and night. I hardly step out of the house. I stay amongst them.

Previously published in Bengali as '*Maya*' in
Bibhutibhushan Golpo Shomogro.

Ghost

What amazing almonds used to grow in Shirish Pramanik's large plantation! The road ran along one side of it. Full of ancient trees of all kinds that had been there since ages. Even during daytime, the heart of the plantation used to be dark and covered in dense shadows.

Just a little distance away is our higher primary school—Rakhal Master's school. There is a huge mulberry tree in the school compound because of which we refer to the school as 'The School beneath the Mulberry Tree'.

There are two teachers in our school. One of them is Hiralal Chakraborty. He has a shop for selling pots quite close to the school; hence he is commonly referred to as 'the-master-who-sells-pots'. He is less of a master, though, and more of a Yamaraj. Looking at the width of his cane makes one break out in a cold sweat. During lunch recess, the masters used to take a nap. Recess basically meant a break for the masters, a break for a long nap. We students roamed around in the fields and gardens as our fancy took us. Sometimes, returning to the school after an hour or so, we would find that the masters hadn't awoken yet. To us, this indicated that the lunch recess wasn't yet over.

That day as well, the same sequence of events played out.

We went to the railway line which is quite far from our school. We wandered around the Matla Bridge and even sauntered along the railway line. When we came back, the-master-who-sells-pots was still snoring away.

Narayan said, 'Hush! Don't shout. Come on, let's go to Pramanik's plantation and help ourselves to some almonds.'

Everyone in our group assented.

I said, 'Is plucking almonds child's play?'

'There are many lying underneath the tree at this time of year.'

'All right, let's go and see.'

So off we went and entered the Pramanik's plantation from the road that passes underneath the bridge. It was two o'clock in the afternoon, and the sun was bright and strong. It was the autumn season; hence the sun's rays were beating down on the fields with particular vigour.

During the previous monsoons, wild weeds and thorny shrubs had invaded the plantation, and at various places along the narrow path leading through the jungle, thick creepers could be seen hanging down from the overhead branches up to the top of the undergrowth. We hadn't been to all parts of the plantation before. It is quite extensive—starting near the concrete road and extending all the way up to the riverbank.

We saw guavas growing on some trees, but they hadn't yet attained their full size and form. Searching to see if we could find fruits of other kinds, we almost reached the riverbank. We didn't find many almonds. We found a few, but I for one didn't have the patience to stop and work on them, cracking their shells with stones to take out the kernel. Consequently, I gradually lost track of the rest of the group. Towards the riverbank, the jungle is extremely dense. Hardly anyone comes this way.

I could hear the sound of a fox ambling over the dry leaves somewhere in the forest. A bird was calling out from the top of a tall tamarind tree. Alone, I started feeling somewhat afraid.

The boys at our school often put their hands to their ears and sing loudly:

Right at noon
The ghost gives a shove,
The ghost's name is Roshi,
Let's sit down with our knees close-up!

And promptly they flop down and sit with their knees close together. It is said that this is a good remedy to save yourself from ghosts and remove their fear from your heart.

Well, there's no one with me right now, and it is noontime! Should I chant the mantra and sit down with my knees up close and together? But why should the ghost's name be Roshi? It could just as well have been Shyam, or Kalo, or Nibaron.

Turning a corner, I entered a stretch of bamboo forest with dense undergrowth. Then I saw something that almost made my heart stop beating.

Some distance away, underneath an *amra* tree, was *Boro-Bagdini* sitting with her back resting against the bole of the tree. I took a good look. Yes, as clearly as my eyes could see it was indeed Boro-Bagdini. Good heavens! But she is supposed to be dead.

Boro-Bagdini used to stay at Gosai *para* in our village, in a simple straw hut built in the fields underneath the banyan tree. She had nobody to call her own. She used to work as a maid at Pal *Moshai*'s house. Then one day she fell grievously ill. Thereafter, she was not to be seen. That's all I know.

Around two months back, the dead body of a woman was found in the bamboo forest at the edge of the swamp. Dogs and jackals had eaten a part of the body which was thin and dark, just like that of Boro-Bagdini. Everybody said that weak from fever, she must have fallen into the swamp while trying to fetch some water for herself.

And now it was that same Boro-Bagdini sitting comfortably with her back resting against the trunk of the amra tree!

Rushing through the plantation I ran helter-skelter towards the road. When I reached the almond tree where the rest of the group was gathered, my entire body was shivering with fear.

The boys said, 'What's wrong with you? Why are you looking so pale?'

I stuttered, 'Ghost...!'

'Where?'

'What did you say?'

'Nonsense!'

'Boro-Bagdini is sitting there in the midst of the undergrowth! Underneath the amra tree, towards the edge of the river. I saw her with my own eyes!'

'What are you saying? How is that possible?'

'I saw her with my own eyes, I promise you. I saw her clearly. It was Boro-Bagdini for sure.'

'Nonsense! What lies! Come, let's go and see.'

In great excitement, the boys decided to go to that distant spot and see for themselves. But at that very moment Nimai Kolu said, 'No, hold on! If we believe him and go all the way there to check, we'll get really late in returning to school. The masters must have woken up by now. You know that the-master-who-sells-pots keeps a hefty cane and can use it very well! Who wants to invite his wrath and get into trouble? I, for sure, won't accompany you. You guys can go if you want to. Anyway, it's all lies that he says!'

Recalling distinctly the power of the master's cane, the excitement and energy of the boys dissipated. One by one, they made their way back towards the school. I did the same.

When we reached the school, we could tell from looking at the masters that they had woken up just a while back. Chakraborty Moshai was walking impatiently to and fro outside our empty classroom. Seeing us approach, he let out, 'Done with your play?'

We could have responded, 'Sir, you are done with your slumber, are you?' But who would dare? Subjected to his angry gaze, all of us seemed to have shrunk to minuscule proportions.

We'd hardly entered the classroom when he called out loud, 'Ratan!' I forced myself to step forward.

'Where were you boys hanging out?'

I started shivering like a wet owl. It seemed like I'd hardly got rid of Boro-Bagdini when the-master-who-sells-pots got hold of me. I was in a wretched state. But I had a last weapon in my arsenal, which I now released.

I said, '*Pandit* Moshai, the boys know why we're late. Just a while back, when we went to the Pramanik's plantation to gather almonds, I saw a ghost—that's why...'

Disbelief and alarm seemed to appear on the master's face simultaneously. 'A ghost, did you say?'

'Yes, Sir. A ghost. Creatures which...'

'I know what a ghost means, you obnoxious monkey! But what kind of a ghost? And where did you see it?'

I narrated everything in detail. My companions corroborated my version of events and told him how they'd seen me come running towards them, panting and out of breath.

Chakraborty Moshai called out to Rakhal Master, 'Do you hear, brother?'

Rakhal Master was in the process of gathering materials to prepare his pinch of tobacco. He said, 'What's that you say?'

'Listen to the boys. Ratan has just seen a ghost at Shorbo Pramanik's plantation.'

'Who's Shorbo Pramanik?'

'*Arre*! Shorbo Pramanik was Shirish Pramanik's father. It is that same plantation.'

I was again asked to narrate the entire sequence of events.

Rakhal Master was a true orthodox Brahmin. He believed in every kind of superstition. With a serious expression on his face, he said, 'That's quite expected, isn't it? It was an accidental death. The soul hasn't found peace.'

The-master-who-sells-pots was something of an atheist, and one could discern the scepticism in his words when he remarked, 'But brother, can we really expect a ghost to be sitting in a garden at noontime, resting its back against a tree?'

'Why, where's the problem? Is it written anywhere that a ghost is not supposed to be in a relaxed state of being? You people simply have too many objections.'

'Okay, let's go and check this matter out.'

All the boys shouted their assent in one voice.

Rakhal Master said, 'You folks will never learn. You expect the ghost to be sitting there, waiting for you, do you? These creatures are, one could say, bodiless...meaning they are not limited by physical bodies. They're in a...er...peculiar state, you could say.'

The-master-who-sells-pots said, 'But come, let's go and at least see what all the fuss is about. What's the harm in that?'

All of us boys wanted to go. We knew it would mean the end of the day's classes and that would be much to our liking. So we went along too.

Crowding around the masters, we gradually made our way towards the spot. I took the lead, and the rest of the group followed me through the dense undergrowth and wild shrubs. Together, we somehow made it to the spot under the amra tree. I can never forget the sight that met our eyes. Even after all these years, I can still see it vividly before me.

What we saw is precisely as follows.

A torn rag, filthy and foul-smelling, had been placed under the tree. Close by was a small earthen vessel, half-filled with water. Umpteen peels and seeds of the amra fruit were lying around—a few fresh and the rest a few days old. There were also many dry skins and rinds of raw tamarind fruit and ripe elephant apple.

On the torn rag, the worn-out and old, haggard body of Boro-Bagdini was lying lifeless. She seemed to have died a while back.

We went away to inform everyone about it. The *chowkidar* and *dafadar* of the village came to take a look. Who can say why Boro-Bagdini had left her straw hut and hidden herself in this jungle? Some people said that she had lost her senses; others opined that she had been possessed by spirits.

But Boro-Bagdini had clearly died hungry and emaciated, possibly after suffering from malaria that is brought on with the arrival of the *Ashwin* and *Kartik* months. She didn't even have water offered to her in her last moments. Who could have given it to her in this remote jungle? No one was even aware of her presence in this forlorn place.

The answer to the mystery of why Boro-Bagdini had chosen to come here and remain in hiding has been taken along with her to the other world.

Previously published in Bengali as '*Bhoot*' in *Bibhutibhushan Golpo Shomogro.*

In the Jungle of Bomaiburu

Various sections of the jungle are being surveyed. A surveyor of ours, an *ameen* named Ramchandra Singh has been stationed for the past few days in the jungle of Bomaiburu, around six miles from our head office. News came in this morning that two or three days ago, Ramchandra Singh suddenly turned insane.

On receiving this news, I collected some men together and made for the forest. The jungle of Bomaiburu is not very dense. It is an expanse of bare, undulating plains interspersed with huge trees; thin, cord-like creepers hang down from the branches, giving the appearance of ropes tied to the high masts of a ship. The jungle is entirely devoid of any human settlement.

We passed through a stretch where the trees were comparatively dense, and when we came out on to an open plain field, we saw two small reed huts. One was slightly larger than the other. The survey clerk, Ramchandra, stays in this one. The other smaller hut is occupied by his footman, Ashrafi Tindel. Ramchandra was lying on his wooden bunk with his eyes closed. At the sound of our approach, he got up hurriedly from the bunk. I asked him, 'What's the matter Ramchandra? How are you?'

Ramchandra clasped his hands together in greeting but didn't say anything.

Ashrafi Tindel answered our question instead. He said, '*Babu*, there is something astonishing that I have to tell you. You may not even believe it. I would have come down to the office myself to inform you, but how could I possibly leave Ameen Babu alone? The matter is this: for the past few days, Ameen Babu has been saying that a dog comes during the night and troubles him a lot. I sleep in the small hut, and Ameen Babu sleeps here. Every day, he says the same thing: "*Arre*! God knows from where this white dog turns up every night! As soon as I arrange my bed on the bunk and lie down on it, along comes this dog and whimpers beneath it, trying to rub itself against me." I listen to him but don't bother myself much about it. Four days back late in the night he called out, "Ashrafi, come here, quick! The dog is here again. I've caught it by its tail. Bring the stick along."

'Woken up from my slumber, I took a stick and lamp, and rushing out to Ameen Babu's hut, what do I see? If I tell you, you will not believe me *huzoor*, but I really don't have the audacity to stand in front of you and lie. A young woman came out of Ameen Babu's hut and went towards the jungle. At first, I couldn't understand what to make of it. Then when I entered Ameen Babu's hut, I saw him groping about on his bed for a match. He asked me, "Did you see the dog?"

'I replied, "I didn't see any dog, Babu, but I saw a girl emerging from the hut and going into the jungle."

'He said, "You fool! Trying to be impertinent with me? Which woman would come into the jungle at this time of the night? I had held the dog by its tail. I could even feel its long ears brushing against my body. It got under the bunk and was whining. You've started taking intoxicants, have you? I'll complain about you at the headquarters."

'Next day, I kept awake till late in the night. Just as I had nodded off, Ameen Babu called out to me. I jumped out of bed and had just reached the threshold of my hut when I saw the girl to the north of his hut, moving along the fence and going towards the jungle. I immediately entered the forest to check. In such a short time where could she possibly hide, and how far could she possibly go? We people survey the jungle and have the advantage of knowing every bit of the land in this area. And yet, despite searching for her everywhere, I could find no sign of her. Finally, with a sense of anxiety and misgiving, I directed my lamp towards the ground but couldn't see any footprints other than the marks of my *nagra* shoes.

'That day, I didn't venture to speak to Ameen Babu further on this topic. But the incident made me fearful. It is just the two of us staying in the middle of this terrible jungle, huzoor. The jungle has a bad name amongst the people. I am aware of that. I've heard it from my grandfather too. You see that banyan tree in the distance, on top of the Bomaiburu hill? Once, on a moonlit night, my grandfather was returning from Purnia with his earnings. He was on horseback, riding along the forest path. When he reached the banyan tree, he saw a group of pretty young girls, dancing hand in hand in the moonlight. In these parts, they are known as *daamabanu*, nymph-like, evil creatures who live in remote, secluded parts of the jungle. If they find a man in a vulnerable state, they may even kill him.

'Huzoor, the next night, I myself sat guard in Ameen Babu's hut. I kept awake all night, working on survey lists and arranging them. Towards the end of the night, I might have dozed off a bit when suddenly I heard a sound close by and looked up. I saw that Ameen Babu was sleeping on his cot, and some creature was creeping into the space beneath it. Peering under the cot, I was startled to see in that dim light what initially looked like a girl, all curled up with her knees together, sitting there and looking at me smilingly. I saw her with my own eyes, huzoor. I swear to you. I could distinctly make out the thick, dark tuft of hair on her head. The lantern was at the spot where I'd been working on my calculations, about six or seven hands away. I'd just turned to fetch the lantern so that I could see more clearly, when some creature rushed out from under the cot and ran towards the door. The light from the lantern fell at a slant near the doorway, and in that light I saw a large dog, white from tip to toe. Not a spot of black on its body, huzoor.

'Hearing the noise, Ameen Sahib woke up and asked, "What is it?"

'I said, "Some dog or jackal had come into the hut."

'Ameen Sahib asked, "A dog? What kind of a dog?"

'I replied, "A white dog."

'Ameen Sahib said in a disappointed tone, "Are you certain that it was a white dog? Or was it black?"

'I replied, "No huzoor, it was white for sure."

'Not that I wasn't surprised at Ameen Sahib's reaction. If the dog had been black instead of white, how would that have helped him, I could not quite understand. Ameen Sahib went back to sleep, but I felt a strange kind of fear and uneasiness, and couldn't bring myself to sleep. In the morning, I can't say exactly why, but I peered under the cot as if to look for something, and found tufts of dark hair. See, I've kept it with me, huzoor—hair from a female's head. Where did this hair come from? Soft, black, shining hair. On a dog's body, especially on the body of a white dog, one can't find such long, black hair. The incident that I've related occurred last Sunday, that is, three days ago. And in these three days Ameen Sahib has become almost insane. I've begun to feel an unknown dread, huzoor. I'm wondering whether it's my turn now to go mad.'

The story did sound rather incredible. I took the tuft of hair in my hand and felt it but could make no sense of the matter. That it was hair from a woman's head even I was convinced. Ashrafi Tindel is but a young lad. Everyone affirmed that he was not known to take any intoxicants. In this secluded place, devoid of humans and human activity, the surveyor's tent is the only sign of habitation, and the closest settlement is Lobtulia, around six miles from here. How could a woman possibly make her way into these parts in the thick of night, especially given that in this remote forest, owing to the fear of tigers and wild boars, people do not venture out after dusk?

If one assumes that what Ashrafi Tindel narrated was true, then it must be said that the matter is quite mysterious. Or else, one must conclude that in this uninhabited, forlorn and godforsaken place, neither the twentieth century, nor even the nineteenth, has been able to make any inroads, and that this remote part of the country still lies cloistered in the mysterious darkness of a time gone by where anything is possible.

Having their tents dismantled, I brought Ameen Ramchandra and Ashrafi Tindel back to the headquarters. With every passing day, Ramchandra's condition went from bad to worse, until he gradually turned quite insane. He could be heard shouting, singing and talking to himself all night long. I called a physician, but that didn't help. Finally, a brother of his came and took him away.

There is an epilogue to this story. Though it occurred seven or eight months later, let me mention it here itself.

About six months after this incident, around the month of *Chaitra*, two people came to meet me at the headquarters. One of them was quite old, no less than sixty or sixty-five; the other, his son, looked about twenty or twenty-two years of age. They were from the district of Ballia and had come to this region to lease pasture land from us for grazing their cattle in the forest. All other grazing grounds had already been allotted by then; only Bomaiburu was available. Hence, I allocated it to them. The old man, accompanied by his son, went to take a look at the place. He returned looking extremely pleased, and said, 'There is such tall grass in the forest here, huzoor, and plentiful too. *Bahut acchha jangal hai*. If huzoor hadn't been so merciful, we wouldn't have found such good pastures for our cattle.'

I did not, at the time, remember the incident concerning Ramchandra and Ashrafi Tindel. And even if I had, I may not have mentioned it to the old man, the reason being that if he left the place out of fear, it would have caused a loss to the *zamindar*. Ever since the incidents involving Ameen Ramchandra had taken place, the local people had stopped venturing into the jungle.

A month later, one day at the beginning of the month of *Baishakh*, the old man came and presented himself at headquarters, looking enraged, while his son stood cowering behind him.

I asked them, 'What's the matter?'

Shaking with fury, the old man said, 'I've brought this impertinent monkey along to have him judged in huzoor's court. Please give him twenty-five beatings with your shoe. Then he'll be properly disciplined.'

'But what exactly is the matter?'

'I feel ashamed to mention it in front of huzoor, but this ape has become utterly spoiled ever since he arrived here. I've noticed something for the past seven or eight days. I feel hesitant to mention it to you, huzoor, but time and again I've seen a woman leaving his room. There is just the one shack, around eight hands wide and covered with straw, where the two of us sleep. It is not easy to fool me and hide something like this. When I saw this happening on two consecutive days, I confronted him. He acted as if taken entirely by surprise, and said, "What? I've no idea what you're talking about!" And then I saw it happening again over the next two days. That's when I gave him a good beating. Will I watch my own son be ruined in front of my eyes? But despite everything, this did not stop. So I thought it fit to drag him to your court. Huzoor, please chastise him and set him straight.'

All of a sudden, I recalled the matter regarding Ameen Ramchandra. I asked him, 'How late in the night does this happen?'

'Almost always towards the end of the night, huzoor, just a couple of hours before dawn.'

'Did you see clearly that it was a woman?'

'Huzoor, my sight hasn't quite lost its power yet. For sure it was a woman, and young too. One night she was wearing a clean white sari, on another a red sari and a black one on another. On one of those nights, when the woman left the hut, I followed her, but couldn't see where she disappeared into the jungle. When I returned, I saw my son feigning deep sleep. I called out to him, and he scrambled out of bed as if he'd just awoken and was startled by the sound of someone calling him. I realised that the antidote to this affliction could only be found at your headquarters. That's why I've brought him to you, huzoor.'

Taking the boy aside, I asked him, 'What's all this I hear?'

The boy fell at my feet. 'Please believe me, huzoor. I don't know anything about this matter. All day I roam around in the jungle grazing the cattle. By night I am so exhausted that I sleep like a dead man and don't ever wake up before morning. I sleep so soundly that even if the hut were to catch fire, I wouldn't know.'

I asked him, 'Have you ever seen any creature entering the shack?'

'No, huzoor. Once I'm asleep, I have no awareness of my surroundings.'

We didn't have any further conversation on this matter. The old man was very happy. He thought I'd taken the boy aside and chastised him severely. Some fifteen days later the boy came to me and said, 'Huzoor, there is something I need to ask you. When I'd come with my father the last time, why did you ask me whether I'd seen anything enter the hut?'

'Why do you mention this now?'

'Huzoor, I don't sleep so deeply these days. Possibly because my father behaves in that strange manner, a kind of fear has taken hold of me, and I keep alert in the night. Over the last few days, I've observed that a white dog comes into the hut quite late in the night. Some nights I wake up and I see it close to my cot, and then it flees as soon as it realises I'm awake. This has been going on for some days, but last night, huzoor, something strange happened. *Baapji* doesn't know about it. I've come here secretly to tell you. Yesterday, very late in the night, I suddenly woke up and saw that the dog, which I hadn't seen entering, was quietly leaving the hut. The straw hedge in that direction has a gap the size of a window. After the dog had left through the door, within a split second or maybe as long as it takes to bat an eyelid, I saw a girl going past the window and into the jungle at the back of the hut. I immediately rushed out, but could see nothing anywhere. I didn't tell my father about it. He's an old man and was fast asleep. Do these events make any sense to you, huzoor?'

I reassured the fellow, 'It's nothing to be worried about. It's probably just a fault of one's eyesight.' I told him that if he and his father were afraid to sleep in the jungle, they could come and spend the nights at the headquarters. On hearing my words, the boy appeared to be somewhat embarrassed at his own lack of courage and left. But my uneasiness remained. I thought that if I heard of any further incidents, I would send two guards from headquarters to be with them at night.

I didn't quite realise how grave the issue was. About three days later, a tragedy occurred quite suddenly and in an unanticipated manner.

I'd just woken up and got out of bed when the news came that the old man's son had died. Along with a few other men, I immediately left for their dwelling place in the forest on horseback. Reaching there we saw that behind the shack in which they stayed, in the grass and shrubs of the jungle, the boy's body was still lying. His face bore an expression of absolute terror, as if he had seen some strange and fearful apparition and died of shock. I came to know from the old man that late in the night on finding his son's cot empty, he had immediately taken a lantern and gone out in search of him in the jungle, but he hadn't been able to sight his son's body before the break of dawn. It appeared that the boy had been woken up suddenly from his sleep, had seen something and gone out of the shack to pursue it. A thick stick and a lantern lying close to the boy's body indicated that this is probably what had happened. Exactly what he had seen in pursuit of which he had gone into the jungle in the middle of the night is difficult to say, because in the soft mud, other than the boy's footprints, there were no signs of any other creature—human or animal. Nor did the boy's body bear any bruises or signs of injury. No conclusion could be drawn about this mysterious incident in the Bomaiburu jungle. The police came to investigate, but being unable to make anything of it, had left. This incident struck such terror in the hearts and minds of the local people that now no one dares to remain in the forest after sundown, so much so, that should they be forced to venture into the forest out of necessity, they make sure to leave much before dusk.

For a few days after this incident, whenever I happened to be lying on the bed in my room at the headquarters, looking out at the shining white, shadowless, solitary and solemn night, a strange, unknown terror would take hold of me and shake me to my very soul and make me feel that I should flee to Calcutta, that these remote and desolate parts were not safe. Like the nightmarish, demonic queen in fables, there is something here that will tempt you in your sleep and, stealing you away in your unconscious state, will draw the very life out of you. It is as if these parts are not the abode of man but the kingdom of mysterious and sinister disembodied creatures from the world beyond who made this place their own centuries ago, and who, offended by man's sudden, unwarranted intrusion into their secret domain, do not flinch from taking their revenge, given an opportunity.

An extract from the author's novel *Aranyak*, originally published serially in the Bengali monthly magazine *Prabasi*.

Doctor Moni

With the arrival of the month of *Asharh*, the stifling heat of *Jyeshtha* has withdrawn. Thank heavens! What discomfort I had to endure in that heat! And yet, there is not a whiff of air in this *haat*, enclosed as it is on all sides by plantations.

There is nothing that I've been able to achieve at this place either, and it's been almost a year and a half since I came here. But why talk about this place only? I'm almost thirty-four now. What have I achieved in all this time? I have wandered about and stayed in so many places, but nowhere was I able to set up a stable practice or make a name for myself. Bagh-Anchra, Kolaroa, Shimultoli, Shatrajitpur. How many villages shall I name? Nowhere have I been able to sustain myself for more than a few months. When I came here to Palashpara village, my practice did well for the first few months, and I felt as if God had finally bestowed his merciful glance on me. But soon after, things quickly went downhill, so much so that it has been months since I have had any patients.

Now I feel that the time I spent working at Kundu Babu's depot in Shyam Bazaar was probably the best phase I've seen. Someone from my village had helped me get the job. I used to handle documents and accounts. My employers had taken note of my good handwriting and had been happy with me. I worked there for eight or nine months, and in that period, I saw everything that was worth seeing in the city of Calcutta—the zoological garden, the museum, the bioscope, the theatre, the garden and temple of Pareshnath and the Kali temple at Kalighat. What a wonderful place is Calcutta!

When I lost that job, I developed an aversion to the idea of working under anyone. It occurred to me that the medical practice was a magical, independent occupation. I requested Kundu Babu's family doctor to take me on as an apprentice. I spent around two months at his dispensary and learnt what I could. I also purchased some Bengali books on medicine and studied them. Thereafter I left those parts and came to this distant Jessore district, and since then I have been wandering from one village to another.

There are no Brahmins in Palashpara. Amongst the Hindus, there are a few belonging to the *Goala* and *Kolu* communities. The rest are Muslims. There are no well-to-do families here. All the inhabitants are extremely poor and live in straw-thatched huts. It can't even be said that there are all that many people residing in this village. If you ask me why I have chosen this place to practice medicine, the answer will be that amongst all the villages in this area it is Palashpara that hosts the bi-weekly haat. It is not a particularly big market gathering, but still, on Wednesdays and Saturdays, people from quite a few neighbouring villages converge here.

The haat has a few straw huts and also houses the chamber of the Gangulis of Shobaipur. The chamber is also merely a straw-thatched hut devoid of any walls. Once a year when it is time for revenue collection and the scheduled inspection, Zamindar Babu's *tehsildar* comes and stays here for a month or two, does his job and then leaves. Therefore, no one really cares to improve the condition of the room, which is deplorable. The floor is marked by rat holes, during the monsoons the rainwater drips from the roof, and when there is a storm, this inadequate shelter is unable to prevent one from getting wet. Yet I pleaded with the *Nayeb* and have somehow managed to get his consent to take shelter in this so-called courtroom.

I stay alone. Like most of the villages in this province, Palashpara too is lush with forests. On three sides, the haat is surrounded by a dense jungle of bamboos and ancient mango orchards. On the fourth side, a narrow path cutting through a thicket of shrubs, if traversed for one-eighth of a mile or so, takes one to the Betrabati river, known locally as Betna. Due to the surrounding jungle, the haat appears quite dark even during the daytime. After dusk, no one lingers here, and the owners of the few shops that are open during the day close their shops and leave. The haat becomes devoid of all human activity. Fireflies dot the bamboo thickets and wild shrubs once it is completely dark. The *ghentkole* flower, in full bloom, emits a strong unpleasant odour. An owl calls from the *shimul* tree towards the north. All alone, I cook my meal in the kitchen. On some days, having set the rice to boil, I pick up my *ektara* and sing to myself.

It has been six or seven months since I last earned any money. I hung a board at the haat to advertise my presence and practice—a visiting charge of four *anna*s and medicine at a cost of hardly one anna. Even then, there are no patients. Thankfully, Mujibur Rehman is a good man who bails me out now and then, allowing me rice and *dal* from his shop, owing to which I'm still able to sustain myself in this village.

Mujibur is somewhat of a known face in these parts. Everybody is willing to lend him an ear. So last month when there was a case of pneumonia in Damu Ghosh's family at Goalpara, I convinced him to refer me to them. But ultimately Ghosh Babu opted for Balrampur's *Kobiraj* Abhinash, a herbalist, in whose abilities they have infinite trust, I was later told.

Subhashini's presence in my life also presents its own problems. Ever since our marriage, I've had to leave her at her parents' place. I have never been able to give her even a good pair of clothes. There are seven or eight rupees still due to the milkman for the child's milk. My mother-in-law repeatedly reminds me of the expense through letters, but where will I get the money from when I myself have been starving? And because I'm unable to bear any expenses, my mother-in-law is extremely unhappy with me. She is somehow under the impression that my medical practice brings me a lot of money.

No one is likely to believe me if I say that I've hardly eaten anything but rice in these four or five months! Even though this place is but a village, there is hardly any local produce, due to which things are costlier than in other places. *Potol* is two annas per kilo, and potato is six paisa per kilo. Fish cannot be obtained for less than four or six annas. To avoid being seen, I sometimes get up before dawn and go to the riverbank to pick *shaak* for my meals. So many days I've had to make do with nothing but rice and a pinch of salt. It is the mango season now, so my meals consist of just some mango pulp and rice.

So what if I'm not a qualified medical doctor? Can't one read books at home and teach oneself to be a doctor? It has been seven or eight years since I've been in this profession. My experience ought to count for a bit. Don't patients meet their deaths even when treated by trained doctors? When Dhopakhali's Doctor Indu was called upon to treat milkmaid Vidhu's daughter, was he able to save her?

Why then do evil people and mischief-mongers damage my reputation by saying that anyone who takes Doctor Moni's medicine will be sure to die and turn into a ghost? Who can say why I'm being maligned like this? Seeing that I'm poor, nobody takes my side or speaks for me, except Mujibur. If he hadn't been giving me rice and dal for the past few months, I would have starved. No one in these parts has given me a fraction of the help that Mujibur has. I'll never be able to repay the debt I owe him.

This is a remote and backward village. The nearest railway station is almost twenty miles away. There is no big bazaar or *gunj* close by. The people are extremely uneducated. When they fall ill, instead of using the services of a doctor, they try to make do with all kinds of uncertain remedies. Driven by superstition, they say that evil spirits have brought on their sickness. They will often resort to the services of a *fakir* to get Tantric rituals done, but calling for a doctor is not the common practice.

I last went home a year and a half ago. Before coming to Palashpara, I stayed at Shatrajitpur for some time, but even then, I was unable to go to my village. For many years now, I've had no place to call my home, so when I talk of home, it is the in-laws' place that I'm referring to. If I have to go to their house, I must walk fifteen miles to Nabharon station to catch a train to Maslandpur. From Maslandpur, I need to board a bus and travel to Kholapata. At Kholapata, I have to take the narrow-gauge train from Martin Line up to Hasanabad, and from there a journey of six or seven hours by boat on the Icchamati will take me to my in-laws' place. All in all, the travel involves an expense of three or four rupees. Whenever I'm able to save any money, I send it by money-order to Subhashini. If I don't send any money, my mother-in-law and widowed sister-in-law will torment Subhashini no end and render her very existence difficult. Unfortunately, it has rarely happened that I've had a sum of three or four rupees in the past two years.

Last time around, when I was about to start on the return trip from my in-laws, Subhashini called me aside and said, 'Listen, please don't leave me here for long this time. Come back soon and take me away with you.'

'Will you be able to stay with me in such distant, godforsaken, backward, rural places?'

'Do you think this is a town that I'm staying in? Moreover, wherever it is you may stay, it will be good enough for me. Being here and having to listen to *Didi*'s harsh words every day, I sometimes feel like hanging myself or drowning in the Ganga.'

'I understand and I empathise, Subi. If I'm able to settle down reasonably well in some place, I'll surely come and take you away with me. Please do not imagine that leaving you here I am at peace elsewhere. It plays on my mind incessantly. But in my present state, I really don't know what else to do...'

I'd just stepped out of the house when I saw my mother-in-law lying in wait for me. 'Babu, how long are you going to carry on like this? I'm in such dire straits. There are so many dependents in the family that it is difficult to manage. What am I to do? I owe a heap of debt to the Goala for the child's milk. Subhashini has had to make do with torn clothes for so long. Being her mother, how could I see her in such a state? I managed to procure a new pair of clothes for her somehow, but that is yet to be paid for. Once you leave our place you simply disappear, and we never hear from you thereafter! I really don't know what to do. I have never seen such an aimless and unsettled man in my entire life...!' And she carried on scolding in this vein.

It's been a year and a half since that day, and I've never been able to go back and show my face to them. But yes, whenever I've been able to save even a little money, I've promptly dispatched it to Subhashini. But to tell the truth, compared to the expenses I'm supposed to bear, the amount that I've managed to send in all this while is minuscule. But what am I to do? I cannot possibly resort to theft and burglary.

Frankly, from the day of my marriage to Subhashini, we've hardly been able to stay together like a couple normally would. In the early days, I used to think that as soon as conditions improved and I was able to establish a practice, I would take her away with me. But six or seven years have passed since we got married, and I haven't yet found the occasion to act on this resolve. After all, how long can one stay with one's in-laws? As it is, the married daughter of the house has had to stay there all these years. On top of that if the son-in-law stays there for more than two days, my mother-in-law becomes resentful. This is why I don't stay there for long. A person should be intelligent enough to safeguard his self-respect.

One day I heard there was a vacancy for a master at the village school in Pankhola. I told Mujibur Rehman about this when I was at his shop, chatting with him as I often would about the general state of affairs, our hopes and dreams, our trials and tribulations. He advised me to apply for the post.

Coming back to my room, I thought about it. I had given so many years of my life to medical practice, but I still found it difficult to earn a square meal a day. It might not be a bad idea to try a salaried position instead. Whatever its drawbacks might be, I would at least get something in hand at the end of the month, however meagre the amount may be.

On making inquiries, I learnt that Shreenath Das of Makarandpur was the secretary of the school. I decided to leave the next day to see him.

Makarandpur is no less than fourteen or fifteen miles from here. I took a bath early in the morning, ate some rice and started on my journey. I wasn't quite sure of the direction to take. Leaving behind Palashpur, I reached Ambikapur, and found out from the oil-pressers there that if I took the ferry and, going past Jhitkipota, took the route that passed through Nokphul, I could shorten my journey by three miles.

By eight in the morning, I'd managed to cross Jhitkipota. A small boy was my companion on the ferry. When we got off the ferry, he accompanied me for a short distance across some fields and showed me a path leading towards a banyan tree. He said, 'Take this path, Babu. On your left you will see the road to Nokphul.'

The sun was now beating down hard. Crossing a small canal by foot, I found myself in a large mango orchard. A mango orchard in these parts is usually more of a dense jungle than a regular plantation. It took me some time and much trouble to find my way out of the orchard, and when I did, I found myself close to a large house. As I walked along the path that led past it, I was gradually able to make out the successive corridors within the house. Most of them looked ancient. The walls had old-fashioned cornices which were now worn-out and had crevices that had given banyan and other figs an opportunity to take root. Leaving the settlement behind, I found some shelter in the shade of a banyan tree and rested awhile. I had started feeling thirsty now and wished I had asked for water at some household while passing through Nokphul. Being born a Brahmin does not allow me to avail of water at any and every household. Now, further ahead, there were no settlements—only empty fields stretching into the distance.

I set off again. After a while, I began to come across small settlements, primarily of peasants, at regular intervals.

Sudorpur, Chatra, Noldi, Mamudpur.

After I crossed Mamudpur, I entered another empty field. It was past noon already, and my stomach was burning with hunger. It would be nice to have something to eat or at least some water to quench my thirst. Are District Boards in these parts so inept? No tube wells have been installed in any of the villages. Is there no pond in that field I'm walking towards?

By the time I reached the riverbank, via a narrow path, dusk had started to fall. The jetty presented a picture of neglect and was clogged with an overabundance of water hyacinth. The boats anchored there were half-immersed in the murky water. There was not a soul to be seen.

I was clearly in peril. How could I cross the river? There was a village close by, and when I went there to make inquiries, I learnt that due to the invasion of water hyacinth, the ferry service had been forced to discontinue for the past month. I would need to walk another two miles to Khalishpur to get a boat that could take me across the river.

Tired as I was by my day-long journey, it would be quite taxing now to find my way through a difficult path along the riverbank in order to reach Khalishpur. On making further inquiries, I was told that further down the bank there was a spot underneath a giant shimul tree where the river was shallow enough to allow one to wade in and cross it on foot.

It was quite dark by now. After walking for about half a mile, I did finally see a large shimul tree, but the level of water there did not seem particularly low. Nevertheless, I walked into the river. The water was knee-deep at first, and as I moved further into the river it gradually reached waist-level, then it came up to my chest, till moving still further, I was immersed neck-deep. But as I pushed forward, the river continued to rise, and when it reached my nose, I had to prop myself up on my toes to keep going. It was completely dark now, and a fear took hold of me! All alone, crossing an unknown river at this time, what if a crocodile set eyes on me? Even if there were no big *muggers* in these waters, a couple of small ones would be enough to seriously injure me!

Finally, I managed to reach the other side. Peering through the darkness around me, I couldn't see lights or make out any signs of human habitation whatsoever. I could see an opening through the middle of a field leading to two diverging paths. Which one would lead me to Makarandpur—the right one or the one going left? There was no one around to guide me. I finally settled on a path to take, but there was no way of knowing whether it was the correct one. Hard luck usually accompanies me wherever I go. I walked for a mile or so and came across the house of a *Bagdi*. The man informed me that I'd taken the wrong path, and I should have taken the one going right instead of the one going left.

Turning back, I once again reached the diversion and took the path going right. This one had dense jungle on either side—huge mango trees, bamboos thickets that looked impenetrable and all kinds of weeds and wild shrubs. I was aware that tigers lurked in these parts, regularly picking on cows or their calves. I remember I'd once been called upon to treat a patient who had been mauled by a cattle-lifter and had sustained deep wounds on his shoulder.

Walking on the path in the pitch dark proved to be troublesome. It was dotted with ripe mangoes that had fallen from the trees that grew on either side. There is such an abundance of mangoes in these parts that the fruits have little worth, and hardly anyone bothers to gather those that have fallen on the ground. I kept slipping and losing my footing as I stepped on mangoes in the darkness. I couldn't help thinking to myself: as long as it is mangoes that I'm stepping on it's fine, but if I happen to put my foot on a snake, I will need immediate medical treatment in order to survive.

After much trouble, I managed to reach Makarandpur at nine in the night. I found shelter for the night at the home of the secretary, Shreenath Das. But I didn't get the job for which I'd come this far. Next morning Shreenath Das said, 'Not this month. I'm thinking I'll induct new staff in the month of *Ashwin*. The financial position of the school is not very good. Next month, the District Board will help us with an amount of ten rupees and four annas. That is our only hope. We earn a mere three rupees and twenty-five paise a month from the students' fees. How do I keep two teachers? But you may contact us in the month of Ashwin.'

So, even this opportunity didn't amount to anything. But how would I survive until the next month while waiting for the job of second teacher at Pankhola Upper Primary School? I found out that the salary was five rupees. The headmaster gets nine rupees.

I had to walk the whole of the next day in order to get back to Palashpur. Dusk had fallen by that time. I was extremely exhausted, and my legs were shaking. Mujibur asked, 'How did it go, Doctor Babu?'

I told him everything. Thereafter, entering my dark straw-thatched room, I lighted my broken lantern. I went to the riverbank to wash my hands and feet. When I returned, I spread my mat and lay on it. I was famished but didn't have the energy to get up and cook something. To tide over the night, I consumed some mangoes to quell my hunger.

Lying there in the darkness, there are so many things that come to mind. Living alone has been the greatest hardship. There is no one to talk to. This is what pains me the most. How I long to bring my wife. It seems like ages since I last saw her. How I wish she were here with me. When I return home after the day's work, how much I would like to have her sit beside me and talk to me. Then, even amidst all these hardships, we would be happy. But how do I bring her here? What would I feed her?

The haat appears so terribly dark and desolate. There are just two shops, and their owners have closed shop and left for the day. All around stand massive trees, but in the dense darkness, only the fireflies can be seen glowing on the trees. On the *amra* tree, the sound of bats flapping their wings can be heard.

Although it is late in the night, sleep eludes me. This stifling heat is hideous. Lying there on the mat, all through the night I hear the sound of ripe mangoes falling to the ground.

Oh! My life here has become so dreadfully dull. Waking up in the morning, I go for a stroll by the riverbank and then return to the haat. I cannot venture out for long, lest I miss a patient. Throughout the day I sit patiently at the dispensary in the hope that a patient will turn up.

Sitting under the tree, I close my eyes,
Thinking to myself that I can find you thus
But all I perceive is the tremor and longing in my heart...

Where else can I go anyway? It's a backward village and there's no educated person to whose house I can go for a bit of conversation. For me, there is only the dispensary, built of straw and with holes in the floor, and Mujibur's shop. Just these two. The dispensary and the shop. On some evenings, when I go for a stroll near the marsh at Pipalipara, I see Bagdis aboard a *donga*, hunting perch with a spear. When it becomes dark, I sometimes pick shaak for my dinner.

The same monotonous regime of mango pulp and rice has been continuing since the arrival of the month of *Baishakh*. How long can one live on such a diet?

There is no luck to my name! Yesterday, sometime after dusk, in the neighbouring *para,* Bishnu Kolu's elder son was bitten by a snake. As soon as I heard about it, I rushed to their place. It is true that no one had come to call me to attend to the boy, but when I got the news, how could I sit and do nothing?

I tied some bandages on the boy's body to prevent the poison from spreading, made an incision at the site where the snake had bitten and applied some potash permanganate. I'd proceeded thus far when the people of the para brought along an *ojha*. This man ordered the bindings to be removed. I warned against it, but nobody paid attention. By the time the bindings were taken off and the ojha had performed his rites and applied various charms, the boy started to recover. The ojha's rites were superstitious nonsense, of course. The bindings and the potash permanganate had worked the actual cure, but it was the ojha who took all the credit. So be it. I am not sorry. A life was saved, and that is sufficient reward for me.

I endure the pangs of hunger and even the torment that this lonely, dreary life brings every day—a torment that seems to kill me. Despite this, I often daydream and think of what I would do if good times came my way and I had enough money in hand. It helps me to drive away the torment in my heart. I would bring Subhashini and my *khoka*. If Mujibur is willing to give me some land close to the riverbank, I would build a couple of straw huts there. All around the house I would plant a small flower garden. On summer evenings, I would fill a plate with flower buds picked from the garden. I would keep some in the room and adorn Subhashini's hair with the rest. I could request the tehsildar for a small portion of a paddy field and cultivate it. Paddy in the house would lead to sufficiency. And thus, I would dream.

I was sitting in the dispensary one day during the month of *Bhadra* when I saw a girl in the jungle close to the haat, searching for something under a tamarind tree. On noticing me, she gazed at me for some time.

I asked her, 'What are you looking for *khuki*?'

Shyly, the girl replied, 'Ghentkole stalks.'

'What will you do with ghentkole stalks?'

'I will use them in cooking.'

I didn't know that ghentkole stalks were edible. If so, then my need for vegetables could be met, and I would be spared the trouble of buying any. I thought I could see an abundance of ghentkole growing in the jungle around the haat. But I wasn't familiar with this plant, although I knew the name.

I said, 'Let me see what kind of a plant it is.'

Showing me one, the girl said, 'See, it looks like a *kochu* plant. But the leaves are three-lobed.'

'How is it prepared?'

'Any way you like. It can be used to prepare curry or cooked till dry with other vegetables. Will you eat it? Do you want me to pick some for you?'

I didn't give an honest answer to this. Being a doctor, how could I possibly consume some random wild greens? And if I do, it would only be as a favour to these ignorant, unsophisticated plants—that's the impression I tried to convey.

I said, 'Who would want to cook stalks of these wild shrubs? How are they prepared, anyway?'

The girl taught me how to prepare a ghentkole curry, and also picked a bunch of the stalks for me.

Before she left, she glanced towards my kitchen and asked, 'Who lives here?'

'I do,' I replied.

'I mean, who else stays with you? Who cooks for you and serves you?'

'No one. I do it myself.'

It seemed to me that the girl gave me a compassionate look. Henceforth, whenever she came to the haat to collect ghentkole, she would pick some for me as well.

She used to come in the mornings, and then again in the evenings. One day in the evening, I was sitting in the dispensary lost in my thoughts when the girl came to the doorway and taking some figs from the folds of her dress, put them on the medicine chest and said, 'Here are some figs I picked from the tree near Hari Kolu's pond.'

I had never asked her who she was. She was good-looking, had large eyes and must have been around eighteen or nineteen. She was fairer than most people one encountered in these parts. But I could tell that she was not from a Brahmin or *Kayastha* household. When I asked her about herself that day, she told me that she was from the village and was the daughter of a dairywoman named Vidhu, that her name was Premlata (or something of that sort) and that everyone called her 'Pramo'. She had been widowed at a young age, as happens quite frequently in Goala households in our country.

Holding on to the bamboo frame supporting the roof, the girl kept standing there for some time. Then she asked, 'Are you not married?'

'Yes, why wouldn't I be?'

'Then how come you haven't brought your wife here to stay with you? You seem to be having a difficult time with your cooking and other household chores.'

'Yes, that is true. I'm thinking of bringing her this time around.'

'Are your parents alive?'

'No.'

'Where are you from?'

'You won't know the place. It's quite far from here.'

That was the beginning of our acquaintance.

Thereafter, I often saw her at the haat in the mornings and evenings. On some days she would give me *oler danta*, on another day some figs or else an elephant apple. It seemed that if she didn't give me a portion of whatever she managed to collect from the fields and jungles, she wouldn't be content. Sometimes she would stand there holding the bamboo frame and talk to me of many things. A simple girl gathering firewood and edible shrubs, she tried to help her impoverished mother tide over the scarcity of their household. In the same way, out of a sense of profound compassion for this penniless doctor, she used to arrange for something to be laid on his plate.

I liked her very much. I think I was attached to her by a fellow feeling, and I believe she too was attached to me by an unseen thread of sympathy. In my lonely life at Palashpur, her gentle presence was comforting. Whenever she came to the haat my heart felt glad. Lately, she had started coming quite frequently, and on various pretexts. When she came, she stayed for quite a long while, chatting with me.

One day I noticed that Pramo had started taking care of her attire and appearance. The first time I realised this was on an occasion when she had tied her hair carefully in a neat bun. I saw that she had learnt to drape her saree properly and was wearing a clean one that day. In the smile of her face, I one day noticed an abashed and hesitant manner—the kind that was new to her.

She tried to express her care in many ways—picking shaak for me or chopping vegetables. Appearing at the front of the dispensary, she would stand there holding the bamboo frame. Lately, she had begun to sit in the corner close to the chest of medicines. I couldn't help noticing that her face had started becoming comelier by the day.

There are many people at Palashpur, and so many of them pass through the haat, but no one other than Pramo had shown this lonely and impecunious doctor any sympathy. This makes me think that for a man there can be no better friend than a woman.

In the month of Phalgun, she didn't come to see me for several days. I started feeling anxious. This had never happened before. After a couple of days, I heard that the dairywoman Vidhu's daughter had typhoid. Although no one asked me to, I went to see her. On examining her I realised that at her young age, typhoid would probably prove to be incurable. I did all I could to treat her, but after seven days her family lost faith in me and called for Doctor Indu. When I went to see Pramo the first day, her face had lighted up. I heard that when Doctor Indu had come to see her, she had refused to take his medicines. The six or seven days prior to her death, she had been unconscious.

It's been a few months now. I'm again the way I used to be, alone. Who will pick shaak, figs and ghentkole stalks for me now? It's back again to mango pulp and rice.

The rains have arrived. The paths are wet and muddy, and the mosquitoes have increased. Clouds have been accumulating all day long over the huge trees that surround the haat. Some steady rainfall clears the sky a little, whereupon clouds flying in from faraway places again gather on the skyline, followed by more rain. With water incessantly falling, the colour of the tree trunks now appears dark as ebony.

I sit in my room silently, feeling as if I'm incarcerated in a prison. When it becomes unbearable, I go and sit in Mujibur's shop. The shop, built of straw, has a low roof. Castor oil, kerosene, masalas, limestone, raw tobacco, coal-tar, mustard oil—all these together result in a strange odour that always pervades the shop, making me feel slightly sick. Then I wonder what I'm doing in this desolate, nondescript village. Will I ever gain release from this serpent-like noose? Who can say whether I'll ever be set free or not? Life has taken such a strange course. But though I live in so much discomfort and hardship in this faraway place, I can't help feeling that even this agonisingly tedious existence would have been bearable if Subhashini and Khoka were with me.

In the days when I stayed in Calcutta, I was once passing through Bhawanipur when I saw groups of girls with books in their hands coming out from a large house. There were girls of various age-groups.

I fell to musing—what's this that I see? Where do so many girls come from? I need to know what this is all about.

Thereafter I came to know that it was actually a girl's college. Such charming girls! Their attire, the spectacles that they wore, their beauty!

Another time when I was passing through Debendra Ghosh Street, from the second storey of a rich man's house, a girl could be heard singing. I stood there and listened. I've never heard such a beautiful song ever again. Where now would I come across such songs anyway? I still remember a few lines of that song.

Dear, you didn't come this morning,
Even the flowers weep with dewdrops.

Such songs are not meant for simple earthy people like me.

After raining all day, come evening the clouds seemed to have called for a halt. The darkness of the trees combined with the murky sky adds to the feeling of seclusion in the haat. In little puddles of water, frogs can be heard croaking in delight. At the spot where Pramo used to pick ghentkole stalks, crickets have set up a monotonous, stridulating sound. From the tall branches of the *jamun* tree, the ripe fruits can be heard falling onto the wet undergrowth whenever there is a sudden gust of breeze.

In this lonesome evening, I sit alone and think...

Previously published in Bengali as '*Moni Doctor*' in *Bibhutibhushan Golpo Shomogro*.

The Intoxicant

At the time I was working at the Lahore Museum, I was on very good terms with the editor of the well-known newspaper *Deshbandhu*, Vinayak Dutt Singh. Mr Singh belonged to an old, aristocratic family. Their ancestral home was not in Punjab. His great-grandfather had come from the Kota region of Rajputana to Punjab to take care of matters of state. The family had been in Punjab since then. I used to occasionally visit them in the evenings and sitting in their drawing room, look at the various types of armour, axes, spears, banners and other Rajput instruments of war hanging on the walls. I enjoyed listening to the discourse and history related to them. Mr Singh's knowledge of Rajputana, especially the history of the Kota region, is quite profound.

But this is not what I want to tell you about. There is a strange incident I would like to share with you. If I hadn't heard the story from an educated and respectable person like Mr Singh, I too would have dismissed it as a tale of no importance.

One day in the winter, I'd gone to their house in the evening and was sitting in the drawing room. It was very chilly that day. After having two cups of tea, I was enjoying a cigarette (Mr Singh doesn't smoke) when something prompted me to ask him, 'Mr Singh, do you believe in evil spirits?'

Mr Singh thought for some time and then said, 'Yes, I do.'

'Have you ever seen ghosts or spirits?'

Mr Singh solemnly replied, 'I'll tell you of something that happened. Not to me. It's an incident from the life of my grandfather's younger brother. If that event hadn't taken place, our family might still have been living in Kota as eminent and respectable *talukdars*. We wouldn't have been obliged to come to Lahore and join the government service. It was really quite astonishing, that incident.'

I asked, 'In what way?'

'Listen then. My *Chhoto* Grandpa wasn't my grandfather's real brother, but was born of a stepmother. He was a handsome man, fond of the good things of life.'

Looking at Vinayak Dutt Singh's tall, cream-coloured, robust physique I could not disbelieve his words.

He continued, 'When I first saw him, I was very young. But I remember him as being completely insane. Entirely! How he came to be in that state is what forms the heart of this story. By virtue of being insane, the law of the Kota *Rajdurbar* dictated that his portion of property and belongings were lost to the family—but that is another matter. Let's not go into that. Let me tell you what happened.'

In his typically enthusiastic manner, Mr Singh narrated the entire story. I had interrupted him at several points when he was speaking. So, eliminating those intervals let me tell you the story in my words.

Some distance from our village was a military camp of the Kota Rajdurbar. My Chhoto Grandpa (henceforth referred to as grandfather) had a couple of friends at the camp whom he used to visit occasionally to have a drink and a good time. Once on a moonlit night, he and his two friends took it into their heads to go to the Bori river and have a bath. They left the camp on horseback.

In the middle of the desert, the Bori divides into three branches and flows along at a gentle pace. During the period to which this story pertains, the first branch of this three-pronged river had hardly any water, the middle branch had knee-deep water, and the last one, a mile wide, was the strongest, with a lot of water flowing through it.

While passing through the first branch of the river, something occurred to one of the friends, and getting off his horse he lay face down on the sand, and nothing would induce him to get up again. Finally, the other friend and my grandfather left him lying there on the sand and moved ahead. Needless to say, none of the three were entirely sober.

Reaching the last branch of the river or the real Bori, my grandfather noticed that his second friend had lagged behind a bit. Glancing back he saw that this friend, having signalled his horse to stop, was staring west of a particular stretch of sand, a dumbfounded look on his face. Grandfather said, 'What are you staring at?'

Wordlessly, the friend pointed in the direction with his finger and indicated to my grandfather to keep silent. Looking in the direction his friend was pointing, Grandfather noticed right in the centre of the stretch of sand some indistinct human forms—going round in circles! He observed them for a while and saw that they were holding hands and dancing. In that secluded spot, deep in the night, who were these people whose merriment had induced them to come and dance here at a time when no one could possibly see them perform? Unable to make any sense of it and astonished beyond words, the two of them simply gazed at those human forms. Why neither of them tried to go up close I cannot say, because I myself do not know. Perhaps their inebriated state was responsible for what they'd seen, and perhaps they thought so too because they didn't tell anyone of the incident at the time.

Three miles north of the main branch of the Bori river is a lake of extremely saline water named Nahara Nipat, meaning Tiger Lake. Encircling the lake on all sides is a mountain range. At some points the mountain range is a thousand feet high, and at others even higher. Salt and minerals can be extracted from the lake and the mountains, hence, sometimes the Kota Rajdurbar used to give the area on lease to merchants.

One day, around three years after the aforementioned incident, Grandfather decided to go to this lake to hunt swans. He had heard that in the dead of night, groups of swans came to the lake foraging for food. He planned to create a small shelter of leaves and creepers at the edge of the lake and hide there before dusk, the reason being that if the swans noticed the presence of humans, they wouldn't come down to the lake.

All plans were in place, but a few elderly folks advised against it—it is not prudent to go anywhere close to the Nahara Lake after twilight, they said. Why this was so, they didn't say clearly. They only said that the place was unsafe. An elderly *Bheel* named Bhyji was a subject of ours. He said that in his youth, he had been a servant of a *Baniya* leaseholder of the Kota Rajdurbar's salt estate whose salt depot and factory were in the lap of the mountains, around a mile away from the lake. He had noticed that late in the night the sky above the lake would light up as if it was daytime, and a strange sound could be heard emanating from the waters of the lake. No one ventured to go near the lake at night. The local people had for long held the belief that this was risky and unwise. Once a cattle-herder had spent the night at the edge of the lake; he was found in the morning, wandering absently around the salt depot. He had gone insane.

My grandfather wasn't the kind of person to lend credence to such tall tales. He only understood and believed in merriment, *shikar* and excitement. He was willful and audacious. He decided that he must go and see for himself.

The aged Bheel told him, '*Huzoor*, if the flock of swans descends to the lake, then it will mean that there is nothing to fear that particular night.'

Grandfather asked, 'Fear what? A tiger?'

'Could be an animal even more dangerous than that. What do I know, huzoor? I can only tell you what I've heard.'

'Why don't you stay with me? I will give you *baksheesh*.'

'Please forgive me, huzoor. Who would dare spend a night at the edge of Nahara Nipat even for a sum of hundred rupees? Don't I fear for my life? We are Bheel. We are not afraid of tigers—with these very hands, so many tigers have I shot down with arrows. But huzoor, is there no creature in this world more dangerous than the tiger?'

My grandfather wasn't familiar with Nahara Lake. It is not exactly in our region but at a distance of forty miles from our village. He left the village of the Bheels, and walking seven or eight miles, crossed over the mountain range and arrived in the plains.

The huge lake could be seen from a distance, its expanse of saline water shining bright under the harsh rays of the sun. No human could be seen all around.

A significant part of the day was still at hand when Grandfather reached the edge of the lake and created a cover of sorts for himself with reeds and dry grass to keep him and his gun well hidden. The flock of swans should not detect his presence.

Gradually the evening deepened. The last golden rays of the sun had faded on the distant slopes. A flock of green parakeets alighted briefly at the edge of the water and took off again. A beautiful moon rose above the mountains to the east. It was the dark night of *Krishna-Paksha*.

The silent, secluded desert all around—and in its midst, the lake.

A couple of hours later the moon shone on the heart of the lake—the bright moonlight of *Krishna-Dwitiya*. Only two days back *Hemendra Poornima* had gone by, and as the night advanced, the cold increased. This beginning of the winter season is the scheduled time for the arrival of the swans. But where were they? Why could they not be seen alighting on the lake?

Grandfather recalled the words of the aged Bheel. If the flock of swans comes down to the lake, then it should be understood that the night will pass by safely. But if they did not come, what danger should one expect, Grandfather wondered? Did tigers come down to the lake to drink?

The night gradually grew dense. The stunning beauty of the lake in the middle of the sandy desert had assumed a mysterious appearance. There was not a sound to be heard. Even though Grandfather was sufficiently spirited, looking at the untouched, preternatural beauty of that moonlit night a strange fear grew in his heart. Taking out his leather flask he took a drink.

All of a sudden, glancing towards the western shore of the lake, he was overjoyed—a flock of swans could be seen descending from the night sky. The moon shining on their milky-white wings made for a breathtaking sight! Descending slowly towards the lake, they alighted and settled down on the sands by its edge.

The spot where they alighted was around two hundred yards or more from where Grandfather was hiding. From that distance, it wasn't possible to get a good shot, especially in the night. Grandfather decided he would wait to see whether they would come a little closer, or whether more flocks of swans would follow this lot. For a *shikari*, there is no quality more critical than patience. He decided to keep a close eye on the birds. But the very next moment, Grandfather rubbed his eyes in astonishment. Yes, he had drunk some alcohol, but was that reason enough for him to lose all his senses, or start seeing such unbelievable things?

Whether you want to believe the sequence of events that followed is up to you, Mr Banerjee, but I've heard this story from my father many a time. It is an incident that occurred in our own family therefore, at the very least, please do not think that I've concocted the story myself. Grandfather saw that these birds were not ordinary swans. They were much larger in size, quite huge in fact. Their mannerisms were also not like those of ducks and swans. As he watched, he felt that they were not birds at all—they seemed almost human in appearance. Grandfather rubbed his eyes again. How on earth could he be seeing things with only a little bit of drink in him? The next instant, the creatures entered the water and swam up close to where he was hiding. The night, awash with the light of Krishna-Dwitiya, revealed to my astonished and intoxicated grandfather that the creatures were indeed no swans—but a group of extremely beautiful maidens! They were well-proportioned like swans. Their white bodies shone brightly in the moonlight. Their laughter, their faces, their movements, in fact everything about them was immeasurably beautiful. For a while they played in the water, and then they started swimming in the heart of the lake silently and gracefully. After some time—how much time exactly had elapsed cannot be said, because Grandfather had lost all sense of time—they rose from the water and, within what seemed like moments, floated away into the moonlit sky, flapping their white swan's wings, and disappeared over the horizon. The air by the edge of the lake was still heavy with the sweet smell of their bodies.

Grandfather pinched himself to make sure that he was awake. By then, he was no longer in a state of inebriation. In a little while, with the sun's first rays appearing on the horizon, night gave way to day. His mind still greatly agitated, Grandfather walked along the edge of the lake and into the lap of the mountains. From there he went to the village of the Bheels.

The old Bheel Bhyji asked him, 'Huzoor, did the swans descend to the lake yesterday?'

Grandfather lied to him. He said that the swans had indeed come, but that he hadn't been able to shoot any.

Now listen to why he lied.

An overwhelming temptation had taken hold of him since noon. He felt he just had to go back to Nahara Lake again that night. If he told Bhyji the truth, the old man might try to prevent him from going.

But that night a flock of wild swans alighted on the lake. A flock of real swans.

Subsequently, for many consecutive nights, flocks of wild swans came down to the edge of the lake, foraged for food, and played amongst themselves. Grandfather kept lying in the shelter he had built, watching the birds. He did not take a shot at them.

Then one night, in the last hours of darkness, instead of wild swans, there descended on the lake that group of mysterious creatures.

This time they ventured even closer. Like wild swans they went swimming in the water, close to the reeds and water lilies, and as they swam by, their unusual and ethereal beauty presented itself to Grandfather's fascinated gaze innumerable times. The moon was still shining although there wasn't much time left for the day to dawn. I can't say what came over Grandfather. Perhaps he was intoxicated or perhaps he was sober, but leaving his hiding place he suddenly rushed towards the edge of the water. I guess he intended to catch hold of one of them. As soon as he emerged and began to move towards the lake, the group of unearthly creatures, like alarmed swans, scrambled to get away, and in the next moment, their white shapes floating away in that evanescent moonlight receded from view and disappeared over the horizon.

The next afternoon, a couple of fishermen found my grandfather on the stretch of sand near the lake roaming about aimlessly, in a state of insanity. They brought him to the village of the Bheels. Old Bhyji shook his head and said, 'I told him that the night the swans do not alight on the lake is perilous.'

Since that time, Grandfather would regain his sanity intermittently, only to lose it again. During the intervals when he was in his senses, he would narrate the sequence of events, not once but many times. In the last ten years of his life, he did not see any days of sanity, and when he died, he was a complete mental wreck.

Vinayak Dutt Singh concluded his story.

I said, 'A most curious incident indeed, but...'

'...But hard to believe in this twentieth century. Yes, I too am aware of that, Mr Banerjee. Even in our own part of the country, not everybody believes it. The events I narrated occurred fifty years back. Some say it was due to the excessive consumption of alcohol that Grandfather's mind played tricks on him, and that he imagined wild swans to be celestial nymphs. Others disagree and say that it is the sight of those celestial nymphs that drives a man mad. That's what old Bheel Bhyji used to say. How can I say which is the truth, and which is not? I wasn't even born then.'

Previously published in Bengali as '*Arok*' in *Bibhutibhushan Golpo Shomogro*.

Glossary

aamloki: (*Phyllanthus emblica*) also known as *amla*, a deciduous tree that bears greenish-yellow flowers, and edible fruit which are sour and astringent in taste and are used in pickles, preserves and traditional medicine.

Ahalya: in Hindu mythology, sage Gautama's wife who was cursed to become a stone and remain invisible to the world; she regains her human form after many ages when Lord Rama's foot brushes against her; considered to be an instance of divine grace.

aloo bhat: a typical Bengali side dish of mashed potatoes with rice and *ghee* or mustard oil.

ameen: an official of minor rank in the judicial and revenue departments.

amra: (*Spondias mombin*) the hog plum, a small deciduous tree native to the tropical Americas, including the West Indies; naturalised in the Indian subcontinent, the tree bears edible fruit that have a sharp taste. The flowers bloom January to May and are sweet-scented, in large, lax terminal panicles of small white flowers.

anna: a currency unit used in colonial India, equal to 1/16th of a rupee.

Annapurna's Charity: an avatar of Goddess Parvati, Annapurna is the goddess of food and plenty in Hinduism; the oleograph referred to in the story 'A Day' is one depicting her thus.

arjun: (*Terminalia arjuna*) a large deciduous tree reaching a height of 60–85 feet, with yellow flowers and conical leaves. Its leaves and flowers are offered to Lord Vishnu and Lord Ganapati.

arre!: an exclamation used to express annoyance, surprise or interest.

asana: a mat which serves as the seat of a sadhu or yogi.

asan: (*Terminalia elliptica*) the *saaj* or *asna* tree, which grows up to 30 metres, and has the remarkable attribute of storing water in the dry season.

Asharh: a month in the Hindu calendar that corresponds with June/July in the Gregorian calendar, and the first two months of the monsoon season.

Ashwin: the sixth month in the Bengali calendar, in which several major religious festivals take place, it corresponds to September/October in the Gregorian calendar.

baapji: Hindi for father.

baba: father; also an affectionate address for someone much younger than oneself.

babu: a form of address which, like *moshai*, roughly translates as Mr or Sir. It may also be used as an affectionate address for one much younger than oneself, as in the story 'Grandma'. In British India, it referred to an Indian clerical employee with knowledge of English, and often disparagingly used to refer to any culturally Anglicised, English-speaking Indian.

Baishakh: the first month in the Bengali calendar marking the beginning of summer, from the second half of April to the first half of May.

bajra: (*Pennisetum glaucum*) pearl millet, grown in the Indian subcontinent since prehistoric times.

baksheesh: in parts of Asia, a small sum of money given as tip.

bagan: a garden or plantation.

Bagdi: an indigenous people found in West Bengal and Bangladesh, and (conventionally) considered a low Hindu caste.

Bahut accha jangal hai: Hindi for 'It is a very good jungle'.

Baniya: traditionally, a community of merchants, bankers, moneylenders and dealers in grains or spices.

basti: a small settlement.

bats: the species referred to in the story 'The Medal' is the Indian flying fox (*Pteropus giganteus*) or the greater Indian fruit bat. One of the largest bats in the world, its wingspan ranges from 1.2–1.5 metres; it is mostly nocturnal, leaving the roost 20–30 minutes after sunset. The gigantic flying fox gliding through the sky, singly or in pairs, is an unforgettable sight.

ber: (*Ziziphus mauritiana*) the Indian plum or jujube is a tropical tree bearing white or greenish-white flowers and edible fruit.

Bhadra: a month in the Hindu calendar that corresponds to August/September in the Gregorian calendar.

Bhairav Sthan: in Shaivism and Hinduism, Bhairav is a fierce manifestation of Lord Shiva associated with annihilation. In the story 'The Mountains of Kushal', it is a holy place associated with Bhairav; *sthan* is Hindi for 'place'.

Bheel (or *Bhel*): a tribal community living mainly in Tharparkar or Thar District of Sindh province in Pakistan, and other parts of Sindh and Rajasthan in India.

bigha: a traditional unit of measurement of land in the Indian subcontinent. The size of a bigha varies considerably from place to place, ranging from 1,500 to 6,771 square metres.

Birhor: an Adivasi forest-dwelling people living primarily in the state of Jharkhand. They speak Birhor, which belongs to the Munda group of languages. Birhor literally means jungle people—*bir* means jungle, *hor* means men. The Birhors are of short stature, long head, wavy hair, and broad nose. Birhors number around 10,000.

Boro-Bagdini: a woman of the Bagdi caste is known as Bagdini; *boro* means elder or elderly.

boro jethima: paternal uncle's (elder to one's father) wife. The term may commonly be used to refer to women who are equivalent in relation.

boro mama: elder maternal uncle.

bouma: daughter-in-law.

Brahma (or *Brahman*): the all-pervading Divine Soul; the Absolute spirit.

brahmagya: one having knowledge of God.

cattle-lifter: when a wildlife habitat is degraded, causing a reduction in the population of their natural prey, tigers are occasionally driven to taking cattle; hence the term.

Chaitra: the first month in India's national civil calendar and the last month in the Bengali calendar, it is associated with the coming of spring.

chhoto ma: *chhoto* means younger, *ma* is mother; in the story 'Grandma', Ramlal uses the term to address his father's younger co-wife.

chowkidar: a watchman, caretaker or gatekeeper.

chuddar: a large sheet or piece of cloth.

conch shell: used in Hindu rituals, its sound is associated with the sacred syllable Om, believed to be the first sound of creation. It is a symbol of purity, brilliance and auspiciousness.

daalan: a lobby or corridor.

dadamoshai (or *dadu*): grandfather; also a polite or affectionate address for elderly men equivalent in age to one's grandfather.

dafadar: in the Indian Imperial Police and certain divisions of the Indian Army under British rule, a junior non-commissioned officer who was a native of India.

dak bungalow: a government building in British India that provided free or cheap accommodation for travellers, especially government officials.

dal (or *daal*): in Indian cooking, split pulses, in particular, lentils.

dargah: a shrine built over the grave of a revered religious figure, often a Sufi saint or dervish.

dasi: maidservant.

dewan (or *diwan*): a powerful government official, minister or ruler.

didi: elder sister.

didu (or *dida*): grandmother; also a polite or affectionate address for elderly women equivalent in age to one's grandmother.

donga: a small boat.

Dooars (or Duars): the alluvial floodplains of northeastern India, which stretch over 350 km from the Teesta river in West Bengal to the Dhansiri river in Assam and form the gateway to Bhutan. The beauty of the region lies in its dense jungles and its tea gardens.

Durga Puja: an annual Hindu festival dedicated to Goddess Durga, particularly popular in West Bengal. The festival is observed in the Hindu calendar month of Ashwin, typically September or October.

Ekadashi: the eleventh lunar day of each of the two lunar phases in a Hindu calendar month—the *Shukla Paksha* (the period of the waxing moon), and the *Krishna Paksha* (the period of the waning moon). There are usually twenty-four Ekadashis in a calendar year.

ektara: literally 'one-string', also called *gopijantra* and *tun-tuna*, it is a one-stringed instrument used in traditional or folk music from Bengal, especially Baul.

fakir: a wandering religious, predominantly Muslim Sufi, ascetic who lives solely on alms; it is now applied to non-Muslim, non-Sufi ascetics alike.

family: in the story 'The Medal', it refers to the direct descendants of Sudhir's great-grandfather, the man to whom Sergeant Parkins had given the medal as collateral.

ghat: a set of steps leading down to a river, lake or pond.

Ghatoyali: an outpost.

ghee: a clarified butter made from cow milk or buffalo milk, used in Indian cooking.

ghentkole: (*Arum orixense*) the Bengal arum is found throughout India, its tubers are eaten in some tribal societies, and the plant has medicinal uses. It flowers in August and, like most arums, emits a distinctive odour for a few hours when it first blooms.

ghoti: a small metal water pot.

Goala: the community and caste of milkmen.

golpata: (*Nypa fruticans*) the nipa or mangrove palm, it is native to the coastlines and estuarine habitats of the Indian and Pacific oceans. The only palm considered adapted to the mangrove biome, it is unusual in that its trunk grows underground, and only the leaves and flower stalk grow aboveground. The flowers are a globular inflorescence of female flowers at the tip, with catkin-like red or yellow male flowers on the lower branches.

gora: an Indian term for any white person, specifically a British colonial.

goran: (*Ceriops decandra*) a tropical plant found in mangrove swamps and tidal creeks like the Sundarbans, it is native to India and Bangladesh, Thailand, and peninsular Malaysia. It grows as a shrub or small tree up to 15 metres, has white flowers and small ovoid fruits.

gunj: a common suffix / prefix meaning 'treasured place' or 'neighbourhood' in Hindi, Bengali and Urdu; used in names of bazaars, localities and towns.

haat: an open-air market, especially one held on a weekly or regular basis, where farm produce, goods, services and livestock are traded.

he: in the story 'Grandma', the old lady refers to her husband as *he* because traditionally, a married Hindu woman is not supposed to utter the name of her husband.

hetal: (*Phoenix paludosa*) a flowering plant of the palm family indigenous to coastal regions of the Indian subcontinent and southeast Asia, also called mangrove date palm or sea date; the trees grow in clusters, up to 5 metres in height, usually forming dense thickets.

Hinglaj: a famous place of Hindu pilgrimage in Baluchistan province of Pakistan, the shrine dedicated to Hinglaj Mata (also known as Hingula Devi) is venerated by other faiths as well. On returning from Hinglaj, at Tatta, the pilgrim is invested with a *mala* or string of white prayer beads like the grains of a pulse.

hornbills: the species referred to in 'The Mountains of Kushal' is the Oriental Pied Hornbill (*Anthracoceros albirostris*), a canopy-dwelling bird. It is a medium-size frugivore. The plumage of the head, neck, back, wings and the upper breast is black with a slight green sheen.

huzoor: in Urdu, a respectful address for a person of rank or status.

Icchamati: a trans-boundary river which flows through India and Bangladesh and also forms the boundary between the two countries. At the end of Durga Puja, the immersion ceremony in the Icchamati offers a unique spectacle.

jaetha-moshai/jethu/jetha: father's elder brother.

jamun: (*Syzygium cumini*) the Java plum, Malabar plum or black plum, an evergreen tropical tree native to the Indian subcontinent and adjoining regions of Southeast Asia and China; it has deep purple fruits, the seeds of which are used in Ayurveda, Unani and Chinese medicine.

jarul: (*Lagerstroemia flos reginae*), the giant crepe-myrtle, Queen's crepe-myrtle or Pride of India, it is a deciduous tree and is used in folk medicine; its flowers, white or purple, bloom only once a year at the peak of summer.

Jessore: officially known as Jashore District, it is in the southwestern region of present-day Bangladesh.

jhinge: (*Luffa acutangula*) ridge gourd, a popular and commonly used vegetable in Bengali cuisine.

jungle myna: (*Acridotheres fuscus*) a bird of the starling family and a common resident breeder of tropical southern Asia, this passerine is found in both forests and cultivated lands, and builds its nest in tree holes.

Jyestha/Jeshtha: the second month of the Bengali calendar, corresponding to May/June in the Gregorian calendar, the period of high summer.

kadam (or *kadamba*): (*Neolamarckia cadamba*) an evergreen tropical tree native to South and Southeast Asia, with fragrant orange flowers that are used in making perfumes. Kadam finds a place in Hindu religion and mythology and is mentioned in the *Bhagavata Purana*. In north India, it is associated with Krishna, while in the south it is linked to Parvati.

kaka: father's younger brother.

Kalia: in Hindu mythology, a poisonous serpent king who was subdued by Lord Krishna; *The Destruction of Demon Kalia* is a painting depicting the event.

Kalighat: a famous temple in Kalighat dedicated to Goddess Kali, drawing thousands of devotees every day. It is one of the fifty-one Shakti Peethas.

kalmegh: (*Andrographis paniculata*) an herbaceous and bitter medicinal plant.

kanda: (*Ipomoea batatas*) sweet potato is a dicotyledonous plant of the bindweed or morning glory family. Petals are lavender to pale purple or white, forming a trumpet shape up to 7 cm long, often darker in colour inside the tube; known to commonly occur in the forests of Ranchi district in Jharkhand.

Kartik: the seventh month in the Bengali calendar, beginning mid-October of the Gregorian calendar, it marks the start of the dry season.

Kavirmanishi paribhu swayambhu: from a hymn in the *Ishavasya Upanishad* which conveys that: 'He is all-pervasive; resplendent; bodiless; scatheless; pure; unstruck by sin; all-knowing; intelligent; transcendent; self-manifest.' *Kavi*: knowing; *manishi*: intelligent; *paribhu*: transcendent; *swayambhu*: self-manifest. The *Rig Veda* further enlarges this concept and addresses the Creator as the Supreme Poet who conceives the grand design and expresses himself spontaneously through his creation. He is the seer, the thinker who expands his consciousness to encompass the entire universe and becomes one with his creation—undoubtedly a most sublime concept of a poet.

Kayastha: traditionally, a caste and community who have worked as scribes, keepers of public records and accounts, and administrators.

keya: (*Pandanus tectorius*) the screw pine bears fragrant white flowers and grows abundantly in coastal lowlands like the Sundarbans, typically bordering the sea. This plant is dioecious, meaning male and female flowers are different and borne on separate trees. This is called the flower of the rainy season.

kheer-sondesh: a popular Bengali sweet made of condensed milk.

khoka: a baby boy or a very young boy.

khuki: a baby girl or a very young girl.

kobiraj (or *kabiraj*): the occupational title of a traditional herbalist involved in medical practice; historically, a practitioner of Ayurveda attached to a royal court.

kochu: (*Colocasia esculenta*) a tropical plant, its edible and starchy corms, leaves and petioles are used as vegetables.

Koel (or South Koel) river: a river that originates on the Ranchi plateau and runs across the states of Jharkhand and Odisha in India.

Kol: used to refer to some of the Austroasiatic tribal groups of India.

Kolu: the community and caste of oil-pressers.

Krishna-Dwitiya: the seventeenth *tithi* or lunar day, considered auspicious.

laddoo (or *laddu*): sphere-shaped sweet made of flour, ghee and sugar, along with other varying ingredients like chopped nuts or dried raisins.

Lakhpatiya and *Daulatram*: Hindi names, meaning one who possesses immense wealth.

log: a Hindi word for people.

Ma: mother; also used as a respectful address for a woman, as in the story 'Kashinath's Tale'.

Ma Lakshmi: Lakshmi is the Hindu goddess of wealth, fortune and prosperity. In India, Lakshmi or Ma Lakshmi is also used to address young girls or the women of the household.

madar: (*Erythrina variegata*) the Indian coral tree or tiger's claw, also known as *mandara*, is native to tropical and subtropical regions, and has dense clusters of attractive scarlet or crimson flowers. The tree can reach 60 feet in height and spread up to 20 feet. It has stout branches armed with black tiger's claw spine and curved prickles on its long leaf stalks. It is said to be one of the five trees (*Panchavriksha*) that adorn Lord Indra's garden in *Swargaloka* (Heaven). The flowers are used in the worship of Lord Vishnu and Lord Shiva.

Madrasi: a demonym frequently used for people, language and things from Chennai (formerly Madras) and the entire south Indian region, typically by those living outside this region.

mahua tari: an alcoholic drink made from fermented flowers of the *mahua* (*Madhuca longifolia*), a tropical tree found largely in central and north Indian plains and forests. The tree is considered a boon by the native forest-dwelling tribes because of its many uses. The flower is edible and also used for medicinal purposes.

mala: a string of prayer beads.

mama: maternal uncle; also used to refer to mother's male cousin.

mandap: a temporary platform built for wedding and religious ceremonies; in the story 'Grandma', primarily for the worship of Goddess Durga.

mantra: a sacred utterance, a numinous sound, a syllable, word or phonemes, or group of words in Sanskrit believed by practitioners to have psychological and/or spiritual powers. A mantra may or may not have a syntactic structure or literal meaning.

Marwari: an ethnolinguistic group, and traditionally a business community, in India and Nepal that originates from the Marwar-Shekhawati-Jaipur region of Rajasthan and Haryana.

moshai: a typical Bengali form of address which, like *babu*, roughly translates as Mr or Sir.

mugger: (*Crocodylus palustris*) the marsh crocodile inhabits freshwater lakes, rivers and marshes, and prefers slow-moving, shallow waters; found in southern Iran, Pakistan, Nepal, India and Sri Lanka.

Munda: an Austroasiatic ethnic group and one of India's largest scheduled tribes, concentrated in the states of Jharkhand, Odisha and West Bengal, and parts of Bangladesh. They speak Mundari, which belongs to the Munda subgroup of Austroasiatic languages.

nagra: a style of handcrafted embroidered leather footwear made by artisans in South Asia, also known as *mojari*.

nayeb: the immediate subordinate of a *tehsildar*.

ojha: a traditional witch doctor who heals the sick, or possessed, through prayer or supernatural power.

oler danta: (*Amorphophallus paeoniifolius*) the elephant foot yam or whitespot giant arum, a tropical tuber grown primarily in South Asia, Southeast Asia, Africa and the tropical Pacific islands. Also called *ol kochu*, it is a commonly eaten vegetable in Bengal.

paan: (from Sanskrit *parna* or 'leaf') areca nut, slaked lime and varying other ingredients folded into a betel leaf, widely consumed throughout South and Southeast Asia for its stimulant and psychoactive effects.

pandit: a priest, teacher or learned person.

para: a neighbourhood or locality, usually characterised by a strong sense of community.

Pareshnath: a Jain temple dedicated to the twenty-third Jain Tirthankara, and a major tourist attraction in Kolkata.

peeri: a small, low wooden stool. In the story 'Grandma', the reference is to its use in *bodhu boron*, a post-wedding ceremony to welcome the bride to her in-laws' home. When the bride reaches the groom's house, a dish full of *alta* or a red dye of lac and milk is placed on a peeri, the bride stands on it, then enters the house with the groom after being welcomed by the mother-in-law.

Phalgun: the twelfth month of the year in India's national civil calendar that roughly corresponds with February / March in the Gregorian calendar.

pir: a title for a Sufi saint or spiritual guide.

poornima: the night of the full moon.

potol: (*Trichosanthes dioica*) pointed gourd, a summer vegetable cultivated and consumed in every part of Bangladesh and West Bengal.

pukka shikari: a real or true hunter.

Rai Bahadur: a title of honour bestowed for service to the British Empire; *rai* means prince, and *bahadur* means brave or most honourable.

Rajdurbar: royal court; court of justice.

Ram-Ram: Ram is a major deity in Hinduism. Uttered twice—Ram-Ram—it is used as a greeting over much of northern India, or as an exclamation variously denoting fear, surprise, disgust or censure.

rishi: a Hindu sage. The post-Vedic tradition of Hinduism regards rishis as *jogis* or great sages who, after intense meditation (*tapas*), realised the supreme truth and eternal knowledge, which they composed into hymns.

sabai: (*Eulaliopsis binata*) a perennial plant belonging to the grass family that grows in many Asian countries; also called *bhabhar* in India.

sandesh (or *sondesh*): a popular Bengali dessert created with milk and sugar, and sometimes cottage cheese.

sal: (*Shorea robusta*) an evergreen tree native to the subcontinent and an important source of timber in India.

Santhal: an ethnic group, the largest indigenous tribe in the Jharkhand state of India, also found in the states of Assam, West Bengal, Bihar and Odisha. The Santhals mostly speak Santhali, an Austroasiatic language, and their traditional occupation revolves around the forests in which they reside. The Santhals worship Marang-Buru or Marang-Bonga, the Sun God, as the supreme deity along with other spirit deities. A characteristic feature of a Santhal village is a sacred grove (known as the *Jaher* or Santhal *Sthal*) on the village outskirts where they believe many spirits live, and where a series of annual festivals takes place.

sanyasi: *sanyasa* (or *sannyasa*) is a form of asceticism marked by the renunciation of material desires and prejudices, represented by a state of disinterest and detachment from wordly existence, for the purpose of living a simple, peaceful, spiritual life inspired by a love of the divine. An individual in sanyasa is known as a sanyasi (male) or *sanyasini* (female).

Sealdah: a prime hub in central Kolkata where one of the two main interstate railway stations in the city is located.

shaak: any edible green leafy vegetable.

shaboo: sago, a food rich in starch and carbohydrates extracted from the sago palm, and used in many popular Indian dishes.

shankha: a white shell bangle traditionally worn by married Bengali Hindu women, along with *pola*, a red lac bangle, and *loha*, a thin iron bangle; all three must be removed once a woman is widowed.

shastra: a Sanskrit word that means precept, rules, manual, compendium, book or treatise, it can be used as a suffix for technical or specialised knowledge in a defined area of practice.

shikar: game hunting as a sport; a *shikari* is a professional hunter.

shimul: (*Bombax ceiba*) the red silk-cotton tree is a deciduous Asian tropical tree with a straight, tall trunk, and loses its leaves in winter. Large red flowers with five petals appear in the spring, and colour the landscape distinctively. The tree grows to an average height of 20 metres, with old trees growing up to a massive 60 metres in wet tropical regions.

shiuli: (*Nyctanthes arbor-tristis*) the night-flowering jasmine, also known as *harsingar*, is native to South Asia and bears small, white fragrant flowers; it is the official flower of West Bengal.

shloka: a category of verse line developed from the Vedic Anustubh poetic metre which dominates classical Sanskrit poetry; it is the basis of Indian epic verse.

Shravan: the fifth month of the Hindu calendar—beginning late July from the first day of the full moon and ending in the third week of August, the day of the next full moon—important as it heralds the arrival of the southwest monsoons in the subcontinent.

Shri: a polite form of address and prefix equivalent to 'Mr'.

Shukla Navami: the ninth *tithi* (or lunar day), said to be ruled by Saraswati, the Hindu goddess of knowledge, music, arts, wisdom and learning.

Shyama Puja: also known as Kali Puja, it is celebrated in worship of Goddess Kali and, along with Durga Puja, is the biggest festival in Bengal and Assam.

talukdar (or *taluqdar*): in Bengal, a hereditary title, next to a *zamindar* in extent of land control and social status; elsewhere in India the powers and influence of a talukdar vary, depending on the region and the period.

tandav: the divine cosmic dance performed by Lord Shiva.

Tantra shastra: a doctrine of enlightenment that combines esoteric elements of Hinduism, Buddhism and paganism including occult, magical and mystical elements like *mantras* and *mudras*. Rather than one coherent system, Tantra is an accumulation of practices and ideas wherein rituals are the main focus. A *Tantric* is a practitioner of Tantra.

tantra-mantra: the occult arts.

Tarakeshwar: a city and municipality in the Hooghly district of West Bengal, it is 56 km away from Kolkata and is a place of pilgrimage and a centre of the Shaiva sect.

tehsildar: a person in charge of collecting land revenue and taxes.

tiger fern: (*Acrostichum aureum*) also known as the golden leather fern, swamp fern or mangrove fern, it is a large species of fern that grows in mangrove swamps and other wet locations. It has large fronds growing to a length of 6 feet, and is tolerant of raised salinity levels.

tulsi: (*Ocimum sanctum*) the holy basil, native to the Indian subcontinent, is a sacred plant for Hindus and traditionally planted in the courtyard of Hindu houses. The ritual lighting of lamps in the evening during the month of Kartik includes the worship of the tulsi plant.

tumtum: a one-horse carriage, usually two-wheeled and high, with two transverse seats set back-to-back, also called 'bounder' in old British slang.

Upanishads: a part of the *Vedas*, these are ancient Sanskrit texts that contain some of the central philosophical concepts and tenets of Hinduism, and played a most significant role in the development of spiritualism and religion in ancient India.

Vastu shaligrams: *Vastu shastra* is a traditional Hindu system of knowledge which literally means the 'science of architecture'; *shaligrams*, used in Vastu shastra, are black fossil stones characterised by the presence of discus marks said to have been created by the Ammonites.

vermillion (or *shindur*): traditionally worn by married Hindu women along the parting of their hair.

Vishwakarma Puja: a celebration of the Hindu god Vishwakarma who is considered the divine architect and carpenter. He is credited with *Sthapatya Veda*, the ancient Indian science of mechanics and architecture.

Yamaraj: in Hinduism, Yama is the lord of death.

zamindar: in pre-independent India, a hereditary title for a landowner who leased land to peasants and agricultural labourers, exercised enormous control over them, and collected taxes from them on behalf of the imperial courts.